A Medley of
International Short Stories

TERESA COSCO HESLOP

authorHOUSE®

AuthorHouse™
1663 Liberty Drive
Bloomington, IN 47403
www.authorhouse.com
Phone: 1-800-839-8640

Published by AuthorHouse 6/18/2012

ISBN: 978-1-4685-5151-8 (e)
ISBN: 978-1-4685-5153-2 (sc)

Library of Congress Control Number: 2012902621

Dedication

These stories are dedicated to my parents
Pasquale and Rachele Cosco
For the love and nurturing that they
gave to their big family,
and the sacrifices they made to
improve the families future.
My thanks to my husband, who
read and made suggestions
which I incorporated into the stories.

Contents

An Adventure in Cooking

Narete is a borough of a very industrious city of North Italy. It was a small area. During the day it was mostly quiet, but early in the morning and after sundown became very populated. The main road, Belfiore Rd., had at one side a very large textile factory and on the other side a pretty large size hospital. Thousands of people came to work in either place in the morning and went home after work at night. The roads were well paved and large. A few trees improved the outlook of the very busy thoroughfare. Almost everybody rode a bicycle. Bicycles were unknown to me at the time. In the beginning I would spend precious time, as I was going to work walking or taking the bus or train depending how far I went, looking in wonder at all those people on their bicycles speeding up on the road. The bicycles were multicolored; the people on them wore different clothing in many colors. They were talking and laughing. At times, the bell of the bicycles would ring for one reason or another creating an atmosphere of cheerful and compelling contentment.

My two younger brothers and I lived at the corner side of the road between Arnate Rd. and Belfiore Avenue in a very small flat which consisted of 2 medium size rooms (one upstairs and another downstairs). We shared the bathroom with another small family. The flat was not big enough for the three of us and the bathroom being in common with another family was a total inconvenience, but after our parents moved north to our city and into the apartment with us, we rented another place that was bigger and better. Nevertheless, at the time, we could not afford anything better because of a misfortune in our family business. I had left our little town in the south a few Months earlier. With the help of our aunt Michela, I worked mornings in a factory from 8:00 AM to 1:00 PM, and I worked afternoons as a fashion design teacher from 3:00 PM to 8:00 PM in Nolamy about 40 Km. away from Terana.

I didn't have time to take care of my two younger brothers who were going to school. At the time Tori was 16 years old and Demi 14. Tori went to school full time at the beginning, and then he had to work in the same embroidery factory where Demi worked. Demi had been working as a young trainee in the embroidery factory for some time. He felt like a confident grown up at his young age of 14. Demi was a quite responsible child, he tried his best to help in any way he could. He was the hardest hit by our financial misfortune. He had to make many sacrifices and he had to endure a great deal of humiliation. Demi always was the most loving of all of us. He is dependable and good hearted. He is of medium height, very thin, and very good looking. He missed our parents a lot. Every time he got paid he would ask me how much more money he had to earn so that our parents and the other two sisters, that were still at home, could come and be with us. I was very touched by his love for our family. At times, I could not hide the tears that came to my eyes, but at that time, I had to be strong for everybody.

Both boys did not know anything about keeping house, let alone cooking. I used to cook for them at night and leave lunch ready for them when they came back home. One day I forgot to cook, maybe because I was too tired. In the refrigerator there was always bread, cheese and salami. In the morning, I left the house before they were awake, and I didn't tell anyone that I had not made lunch for them. For the first time in his life Tori came home from school and did not have anything prepared to eat. He, evidently, didn't like what was in the refrigerator. He found on the table a sack of rice and a can of tomatoes. We kept all the fresh food in the refrigerator to stop spoilage, contamination by bugs, and other unpleasant surprises. He was very hungry and decided to cook some rice. He didn't know how to cook but looking at the rice he said to himself "I can cook this, it is not hard, what it takes is some water, oil, salt, and the tomatoes. When the water boils, I will put in the rice."

He put a pan on the stove with the ingredients that he thought he needed and when he saw the water boil put in a whole bag of rice that was 3 times as big as the capacity of the pan. He diligently stirred the rice. However, "Holy surprise!" Suddenly the rice started rising fast! The pan was almost full and he could not understand what was happening, but he was very hungry. He decided to eat a bowl of rice to make room in the pan. So he got a dish, he filled it with rice, and put in some cold water to cool the rice down. He started to eat, but he had to eat it faster. He quickened his eating again until the bowl was finished, but, by the time he finished the first dish of the rice, the pan was overflowing again. He filled another dish and wolfed it down, but unmercifully the rice kept rising and overflowing. He kept filling the bowl and wolfing it down as fast as he could. He was at his wits end. He was running from the stove to the table filling empty dishes trying to eat as much as he could. Luckily, I returned home from work. As I entered, for an instant, I was speechless; but then I turned the stove off, I put the pan with the still rising rice in the sink, and I tried to comfort my overstressed younger brother. He was red in the face, sweating profusely, and very nearly ready to cry. "Oh Sina," he exclaimed, "I tried not to spill the rice on the stove by eating it as it grew, but the more I ate of it the more it grew." I was ready to laugh, but I didn't want to humiliate my little brother, so I tried to comfort him. "It is all right, Tori, take it easy, you didn't know how to cook and now you do. It has been a good experience for you; do you want to learn how to make the sauce?" "Oh, no! Thank you, but no more cooking for me! I have had more than enough for a long, long time!"

Tori, of all the boys, was the most spoiled, he had a way with words and managed to get off easy in any situation. Tori was known for his winning ways by all of us. My parents had 11 children, the first child, a daughter, died when she was 8 Months old. At the time that I am recounting we were 10 children 7 boys and 3 girls.

My parents had a store that we called an emporium which was a store that was divided into 3 departments, a grocery department, a jewelry department, and, believe it or not, an ammunition and hunting department. "What an incredible combination don't you think?"

One day our father went home and forgot the store keys on the kitchen table, our mother sent Tori to go after father to give him the keys. Tori followed my father to the store but he found out that he no longer had the keys just before he had almost reached our father's store. He immediately turned back looking for the keys on the road he had just traveled, but he couldn't find the keys. He turned back to go after our father to the store where he found that our father realized that he forgot the keys. Our father had gone back home using another route to get them. When our father arrived home, our mother explained to our father that she had sent Tori to bring the keys to him. However, just then Tori entered the house. "Oh here he is!" Our mother exclaimed. "Tori," asked mother, "where are the keys?" Tori very calmly and smiling answered, "I lost them" (Tori was so young that he didn't remember or did not know that: in Italian you say ('ho perso le chiavi' which is 'I lost the keys') he instead said ('l'ho persate' which is 'I lost them'.) Everybody started to laugh. Since then when Tori did something wrong and was not punished everybody would say oh well! It is not a surprise that no one ever punishes him, he "l'ha persate."

Why was Tori almost, always forgiven? He is of medium height, has black eyes and brown hair, he has dimples on his checks and a nonchalant winning attitude with a conciliatory way to defend himself when necessary or to make others feel well. "Was he already a lawyer at 4 to 5 years old?" I wondered then. He is a lawyer and a justice of the peace now. The next is another episode that shows the uncanny conciliatory ways Tori used to put things right especially for himself. When mother was expecting him both she and father wanted a baby girl because they wanted to call her "Mariuccia "(little Mary)" one day while we were having supper and we were talking about the possibility of the arrival of another baby, mother told him "You know Tori when we were expecting you we wanted a baby girl to call her Mariuccia for the name sake of the Virgin Mary" instead we got you and you are a boy. He locked at them for a moment then said "oh mom don't be sorry about it because I can be both. You'll see, when I wear a dress I am Mariuccia and when I wear pants I am Tori. Everything will be OK." We all laughed and went on teasing him, but he was unperturbed and very seriously explained "what do you have to laugh about? Mother is a woman and wears a dress; father is a man and wears pants. Isn't that true?" Everybody became silent at the table for a moment, then another explosion of laughter followed his very serious explanation, only my parents did not laugh, mother took him in her arms and kissed him and said "Tori my beautiful child let them laugh, after dinner I and your father will explain to you why they laugh. Now look what I have made for dessert, your favorite chocolate cake."

We all stopped laughing and started eating the cake. Tori ate his piece of cake with gusto but between morsels he was looking at it in a pensive mood, then he exploded "you are all so stupid." Mother and father did not laugh. Did you notice? Why, do you laugh?" My older brother answered: "Tori wait until they tell you, we are sorry we laughed at you, you are truly still a baby." We were all excited at home because our aunt Rosaria, one of our father's sisters, had a married daughter who was coming to visit us with her husband Paolo. Tori waited with our father at the bus station for them. Tori after meeting our relatives ran into the store to my mother saying, "Mamma, Aunt Rosaria has brought with her a Palo" "A palo?" Answered our mother. "Why would she bring a palo (which is a grapevine support steak) here all the way from Reggio Calabria?" "No mamma, no! This is not a palo of the vineyard; this is a palo that walks." Tori couldn't pronounce Paolo, he could only say palo. Our mother started laughing and said "OK Tori, thank you for telling me. Because you told me I have, now, time to prepare myself for them. When we had a vineyard, we used to attach a long cross or stick to the vines, which we called a palo, to support the leaves and the grapes and keep the grapes standing up above the ground, Also because made it easier to harvest the grapes at harvest time.

Tori had a way of turning his body slightly back and forth, when he had to explain himself. It disarms, almost, anyone of anger or grief. Tori was born when I was a little over 8 years old. Our mother went to the store every day to work, leaving the children in the care of our aunt Teresa. Often, because she could not come to care for us and there was no one to care for Tori, our parents decided to pull me out school to take care of the baby - Tori. I was devastated; I loved to go to school. Now that my life was without school, I wept and complained a lot. At that age I could change diapers, prepare the bottle for Tori, and twice a day bring him to the store to be breast fed by our mother. I soon grew attached to him and he took to me (I believe). In fact, after feeding he would put his little right hand in my bosom to fall asleep. He started talking very early, so much so, that he could not make a distinction between me and mother. He would call both of us mom. I have always been attached to him and (just like all of our family) always ready to make allowances for his actions.

April Fool

After Halloween that year and because after three years I did not get the pay raise that per contract was due to me I quit a job that I liked. It was not an easy decision as I liked the place and the people I worked for. The reason for my quitting the job was my employers hired me at the top of the salary range for my job description. In three years they had relied on the fact that I made more money than allowed by my job description. I did not agree and I said so. In fact, I had previously been told by the same person that I did more and better work that anyone else before me, so I quit. In less than one week I found another job in an elementary school office. The search was not very hard. I read, in the local newspaper advertisement that there was a new job opening that, I thought, was good for me. I sent in my resume and got an interview within three days. This new job was a little further from home than the previous one. The public transportation to the job was long. I had to take, first a BART train then transfer to two other buses. Then I would have to walk a short distance. Enjoying walking to work, I realized that I could forgo the bus travel and walk directly from the BART station. I pondered the pros and cons of the problem and I found that in the end it was advantageous too. I would get more exercise and I would save money too. The walk would help me lose weight. I was happy I had the best of both worlds. I got more money and my exercise as well.

The school was located in an almost rural area that I liked. The building was old and had an imposing façade. I like stately old buildings. They make me think of the mysterious past. It was square and very large. When entering from a tall and large door. The visitor was surprised and could not help looking around to find out where he or she ended up. Soon after entering one was met by a large and long thick stairway. At each side there were two short corridors each brought the visitor to two different class rooms at the end of the stairway. There was a small office for a secretary at the right side the headmaster's office. The headmaster received visitors and took care of all the other endeavors pertinent to running the quite large school population. All around the large void created by the stairway there were spaces allocated to other activities not directly connected to the class room activities? The place was huge there were small and large entrance doors, people, mostly employees, went in and out the doors fast. The secretary who was seated just in front of the stairway readily helped whoever needed help.

One day I waited for the headmaster to finish a meeting with a young student. I, as the new bookkeeper, was stopped and impressed this meeting of the headmaster and a young schoolboy. The boy was seating on a small chair his head barely reached the knees of the head master He with an intent and serious face was listening to the head master who patiently was telling him that his behavior was diminishing his authority. The child was looking at him with understanding but no remorse. I had to descend the stairs and leave as the secretary was looking at me. I never forgot that picture. It registered in my mind with awe surprise and understanding with both parties. At the very beginning I did not like the school or the people that I met. Everybody was nice to me but for an unknowing reason I felt threatened and out of place, may be because the work was somewhat new to me. After a week I felt much better and more comfortable with my work and coworkers. Little did I know that the job would become unbearable and would end in four short months.

I knew that I was a little sensitive about my thick European accent. In this new job environment, there are always misunderstandings when dealing with new people. I knew that and I was determined to try very hard to learn fast and well. I hated to be behind in my work load. I got in the habit of arriving at work a few minutes earlier in the morning to prepare for the day's work. I usually did small jobs like copying documents or filing. One morning I found a sheet of paper face down under the top of the copier. I could see that someone had forgotten to pick up the original. I picked it up to see to whom it belonged. To give it back. It was a flyer for the staff. It proposed to play an April fool joke on the new bookkeeper tomorrow; meaning today. So they plan to play an April fool joke on me? I was surprised. Who would play a joke on me? What kind of joke would it be? Someone wanted to humiliate me on account of my accent, I told myself, "I bet this is the reason." I stopped for a moment, and then I said again. But no, maybe it is just a friendly joke. That day there was a much advertised show of new airplanes up in the sky. I thought to play a joke on everybody in the school. It had to be done before lunch when everybody was in the class room. At about eleven thirty Lucia went to the children's entrance that was on the other side of the building. The classrooms were on the first floor where the large stairway was. Lucia went to the top of the stairway and began to scream "please, everybody come out. The air show has started."

In less than two minutes all the adult population of the school had exited the classrooms and the offices All headed for the outside door. Lucia clapping her hands was screaming, "Happy April Fool's Day, for all, happy April fool's day. There was a moment of complete silence then a roar of laughter could be heard. All the people were talking and laughing while they returned to their work place. For over a week Lucia's April Fool prank was talked about by all. It seemed that no one thought that she could be that daring.

Since the very first week one of the supervisors of

the accounting department was looking very closely at me, to the point that every time he entered the office he distracted me. I would feel uneasy. I did not like him very much. He was tall thin and not good looking I told to myself "Here is another man that thinks that he is God gift to women." I better watch out. My mother who was a very intelligent practical woman, since I was a child she warned me, "to be careful. Lucia", she would tell me, and remind me often enough not to ever make eye contact with men in general as most of them would get the wrong idea. If they do get the wrong idea, they end up by becoming a nuisance. As a habit even now I don't look people in the eye. With this man it did not work at all. Whenever he could, he talked to me or just passed by my office desk smiling. Being busy all the time, I tried to ignore him. I felt circumvented and almost trapped. Then, with dismay and fear, I began to miss him.

My God what was happening to me? "I did not like him at the beginning. I did not like him now. Yet the series of conversations produced a longing for him that I could not explain." I began to analyze the situation and I did not like the results of my analysis. I was almost sure that I had fallen for him; the answer to the question was always the same.

I had fallen in love with a man I did not like or respect. My attitude did not change towards him; I began to look around to find out about him. Margaret was working in the next workstation. She had been working with the school for a few years. I decided to ask her about Tarkolas. At lunchtime, I invited Margaret to have lunch with me. I suggested that we go to a restaurant a little far away to avoid encountering any coworkers. The restaurant was one of the moderately best of the area and we both liked it very much.

When we arrived at the restaurant found that it was spacious and full of light. Each table was adorned with a small bouquet of flowers. The waitress was very pretty and served us almost immediately. While we were slowly eating we began to talk I asked Margaret directly what she thought about Tarkolas. Margaret did not answer immediately, she stood pensive for a couple of minutes, and then she answered. "Of late, I don't know much about his private life. What I know for sure is that he likes women very much. He does not stop at anything until he gets his prey. It seems to me that you have a good mind. Be careful! Make a wise decision. Let your mind decide not you heart." About that time we realized we were already late for work. We left for work and I was sure that Margaret had warned me to be careful and above all not to trust people that were too friendly with me. I cannot deny that I was surprised, but none the less I believed her. I have to confess that a suspicious thought came into my mind. Was she, too in love with Tarcolas? I told myself that it was impossible. She was happily married and older than I was. I decided to cool down and follow Margaret's advice.

That afternoon, after we arrived back from lunch, Tarcolas, after a brief discussion on the importance of a new project, left on my desk a muffin. Everybody knew that muffins were his favorite snack. In that gesture for me there was a message. The first thought that came to my mind was, that he wanted to talk to me. I stood thinking for a moment, and then convinced that there was a possibility that he would say something more direct and explicit to me that would change the already compromising situation for the worse I put the muffin in a small container that was on my desk and marched in his office. As soon as he saw me, his facial expression became friendly, I am not sure, but I think he tried to make eye contact. I immediately began to address him saying; "Tarkolas, you forgot to take you muffin with you when you left my desk." His face changed again but this time for the worse.

Since that day his attitude changed towards me. He was defiant, for a day or so, he was even rude. One day, I found my chair seat heavily spotted with wet substance. I for a few seconds was puzzled. I did not make much of it. I thought that the janitor, in cleaning my chair, had sprayed too much water on it. After a week or so, he began to be nice to me again. I confess that I was very relieved I was almost happy. At that point I was convinced that I did not like or respect him. I was almost ready to change attitude towards him and show my feelings.

The thought of leaving my husband was very hard to consider. I had never thought that I could fall in love with another man, but by then I thought I loved Tarkolas. And that I moved to tell my husband what was happening to me. Something like that could happen to someone else but not to me. How did happen? I was not looking for an adventure or any man. I really had fallen in love and I had to accept it.

That day I was the last to go to lunch. I usually took my lunch in the late afternoon, at about two o'clock. I saw a young man come down from the upstairs offices. He seemed to be was very upset. He hesitated for a moment, then as an afterthought he entered my office and said, "Hi Lucia, I am leaving the company. I have always liked you and I want to say good bye and wish you the best." My desk is near the door and I had seen him, at time, go up the stairs. One could see that he was distressed. So I asked him, "But Henry why are you leaving?" He replied, "I am leaving because he fired me without a good reason." "What are you going to do? "I asked. "Oh, I am painter. I will try to get a student loan and go back to school," "Henry," I said, "I can't believe he fired you. I am sorry to see you go. I wish I could help you," I replied. "Don't worry Lucia. I will be fine," he finished as he extended his hand to shake mine. While we shook hands, he looked into my eyes and said, "Be careful Lucia, he is bad, really bad." He was smiling now, he added, "good luck," and left. My eyes followed him through the door. I stood there looking at him thinking, two people in less than a week had been terminated, they had warned me to be careful. Was I in any danger? The thought and image of our boss came to my mind, and I thought, "This young man may have lost his job because of me". Was our boss telling me that if I would not be responsive to his advances he would fire me too? It could be. Besides he had not spoken to me directly. The doubt and the possibility of a joke filtered in my mind. I decided to wait, at least another week before I did anything.

Two days later I was assigned to do a job that I should have been capable of doing. I tried but I could l not complete it. I just could not put it together. No matter how hard I tried I was unable to complete it. Someone else had to come and help me. I was humiliated and very unhappy about it. What was happening to me? Was I sick? No, I was not sick. I could not concentrate because I had fallen in love with a very dishonest person that was destroying me. But was it really love? I felt a terrible longing for him, but I surely did not like him. I went home carrying with me the burden and the stress of the day. I decided to tell my husband what was happening to me and to inform him that I had fallen in love with another man and that I would leave him. He was watching the television after I told him he stood looking at me in mute stupor. He did not say anything he just stood there. He did not say a word even when I told him that I would file for divorce.

I could not sleep all that night. In the morning I had a horrific headache and a terrible wish to cry. On impulse I fell on my knees and prayed to Jesus to help me. "I am lost please let me see the way to do the right thing, show me the way to do what is just. I don't want to sin. I do not want to wrong anybody. I put the whole matter in your hands. Forgive me, and help me. Thank you." Believe it or not when I got up I felt a little bit better.

Once at work as the usual I took my coat off and marched into the office manager's office. Once there I heard my voice say, "Tania, I quit." She looked at me for a moment then she said okay, let me tell the head master and I will let you know what he says this afternoon. I Left the office in a dream state. I had not planned to quit, maybe, as the saying goes, it was in the back of my mind. However, I was sure I had not planned to quit. But I did. In the afternoon Tania, the office manager, came to my desk. She told me that it was OK for me to quit. She told me that my last day was in a week. I was not happy but I was calm. To my shame I was listening to the sound of the footsteps of people that were coming close to the entrance to my office in the hope that I would see the headmaster enter the door to beg me to stay.

He did not show up at all. I missed him but I was determined to leave him. At home my husband was waiting for me. As soon as he saw me, he asked, "Lucia, how are you? Can I prepare something to drink for you?" I answered, "No, thank you. I am okay. From the door I added, "I want to tell you that I quit the job at the school and that everything with the headmaster is off." I did not want to, but I began to cry. He ran to me and shushed me like a baby. He gathered me in his arms and said, "Please, honey, don't cry. It is not your fault. Listen to me I have something to tell you about this heinous man. He trapped you. He has been doing this to all the women that work or worked for him in the past. He is a womanizer of the worse kind. I don't know if you know that there exists a pheromone that is sold in big expensive stores. I had heard about it, but I did not believe that was true. You know, my love, that this pheromone, no, call it, this love serum, sparks a love response in women's brains. Someone has managed to duplicate it and people with knowledge of chemistry use it to trap innocent women like you. Lucia you can leave me if you fall in true love with someone else but I will never leave you.

After that, I remember waking up next morning feeling sick. I followed my husband's advice and that day I did not go to work. I would have liked not going to work the next day but my husband had been recently laid off from his job and was having problems finding another one. We needed the income. It was very hard but I was determined to resist. I may be presumptuous, but I was sure that Jesus had listened to my prayers and in the end I would be able to leave without any suffering. In the middle of that horrible week, I met the receptionist coming up the stairway. She contrary to everybody else pleasantly saluted me with a mysterious air of importance. She showed me a key saying, "Lucia you know what this is?" She continued without interruption, this is the headmaster's home key. The headmaster is going to be home all day today. She put the key on her desk looking at me to say something I looked at her and without a word I headed for my office. I understood or I thought I did, that the headmaster was inviting me to go to his home to prostitute myself. That was more that I could take. My behavior must have given him the wrong impression.

He must have thought that, I was now ready for it as the saying goes. Was he crazy? I have to say that I may have given him the wrong impression. I was very sad and often tearing. This episode of cruelty and callousness gave me the strength to change my attitude. I dried my eyes and began to act as normal as I could under the circumstances. I went everyday to have lunch out. I initiated discussions with people that worked in the same office with me. The headmaster did not give up.

After that he initiated a long series of shenanigans for my benefit that lasted for years. During break time in a discussion on the subject marriage, I asserted that I believed in marriage and that I never would live with anyone out of wedlock. "But why?" All the people answered in unison. "Because," I answered, "It is immoral, unproductive, and not protective of the children that often are born in this situation. One person is not enough to love and protect them. It is true nowadays that if one does not want to have children; they can just take a pill. We all need love and children are the essence and the outcome of love. I believe that there is no love that can compare with the love of children." No one answered. The break was over and we returned to our desks.

Finally the last day of employment with the school arrived. I was relieved but I also was very nervous. I was afraid that I would cry. I did not. In the afternoon before quitting time, everybody in the office seemed to have things to do outside. At the end of my last day I found that no one was in the office. So I closed the door and left. I had just got home when the telephone rang. The moment I said, "Hello." I heard a loud long laugh. I actually recognized the headmaster's laugh and voice.

Salt versus Fertilizer

*A*t two o'clock in the morning, the Carvels family was awake. The father tried to get the children out of the house because Mrs. Carvels' water broke. She would soon have a baby. The youngest children would not leave the house peacefully because they wanted to stay in their beds. They were going to go to the closest neighbor's house to sleep. In those days women had their children at home. The adults bundled the younger children in blankets. The children left of their own accord and the adults told the young children that Donna Matilda Fairy was coming to bring a new baby. The children knew her as the lady who would reward their parents with a new baby when mamma and dad had been very good. The older three boys would smile wickedly and cough a little. Donna Matilda was the midwife of the town, she was tall somewhat pudgy, she had blue eyes and wore her hair in a bun at the nape of her neck. The children were a little afraid of her because she would threaten them to take them back with her if they did not behave. Nevertheless, she loved children and she would always have a few candies at her disposal to give to them after a successful delivery.

Mr. and Mrs. Carvels had a very large family. They had two girls and five boys the last one, little Cesare had just been born. The first time that Mrs. Carvels ate, after giving birth, the food tasted very bad. She could not understand why. Her sister Teresina was cooking for the family while Mrs. Carvels was in bed recovering from giving birth to little Cesare. Teresina could not understand why the food was bad either. For two days now, there was discontent at the dinner table because the food tasted lousy and no one knew why. Teresina was in tears and was swearing that she had not made any change to her cooking and could not explain why the food tested so badly. Mrs. Carvels because the baby weighed 12.5 pounds when was born, she was still tired and in bed. Usually, two days after giving birth, she got out of the bed. On the fourth day Mrs. Carvels felt better and got up. The first thing she did after nursing the baby was to cook a meal herself to find out why the food tasted so bad. She, also, cooked the meal as the usual, with the same ingredients she used for that type of meal but the meal still tasted bad. Mrs. Carvels wanted to be sure. She called her sister Teresina to analyze the food together, when they got to use the salt it did not take Mrs. Carvels long to start screaming calling her young daughter Debora "Debora! Debora From which sack did you take the salt when you went to the store?"

"From the one closer to the window" answered Debora. Mrs. Carvels screamed, "O my God, my God! Toni, go get your father! Someone call the doctor hurry!" Debora hearing her mother scream, started crying and shaking. She was shaking, because of her mother's screams, she was sure that she had done something terrible but she did not have a clue what was wrong. Debora didn't know what to do, and decided to run away. Once in the street she didn't know where to go, she saw far away a lot of people coming out of the church; she felt safe and ran towards the church. Once inside she thought to make herself small by lying down on a pew. Mr. and Mrs. Carvels owned and operated a supermarket. They sold not only food, but also jewelry, house wares, and even ammunition and other hunting supplies; it was like a department store.

It was the year 1942 so the Second World War was raging. The war didn't spare anyone. People lacked the most basic necessities of life: Everybody was hungry, and wearing inadequate clothing for the very cold winter. The Carvels family did not have to stand in line to get food or clothing from the donations that arrived from America because some of the donated stuff ended up in Mr. Carvels' store for distribution to the needy. Many times when the flour to make bread did not arrive on time, all of them suffered the unwelcome stimulus of hunger too. One time, the children were so hungry that they went to the bakery and stood outside the entrance door to wait for the bread to be cooked. Mrs. Carvels always made pastries for the children putting a little sugar on the uncooked dough, when the sugar was available, to sweeten the pastries. Everyone called these improvised and hurriedly made pastries taralli (donuts). Each of the children of the neighborhood that went to her store got a donut. When the children were hungrier than the usual, they went to bakery to wait for the taralli to cook. The actual baker's oven (called forno [furnace]) was outside the store. Even though the smell of the cooking bread was driving everybody crazy, they waited until the donuts were cooked. When the baker, finally, gave the children the donuts sprinkled with sugar, the donuts were so hot that they had to blow on them and bounce them from one hand to the other until it cooled down enough to eat. All the children were eager to eat them, bite into them, taste the sweet flavor and treasure them to the last morsel. The children were happy afterwards because they could feel strong again. The process of making bread for the store and the family was quite hard for Mrs. Carvels. It involved using a large amount of flour (usually 100 kg). Sometimes less was used, sometimes more was used. It depended on the number of people waiting to eat. Mrs. Carvels, helped by whoever was available in the store at the time, would put the flour in a very long and large container. Then she would put, in the container, the flour, yeast, salt, and warm water. She would wear a large apron and she would mix everything together with her bare hands, after that she would knead and knead a large mass of dough for over an hour. She would cover the whole thing with warm blankets for three more hours for the dough to rise. At times, Debora would ask her mother if she could give to her and to other siblings a little dough to roast on the fire in the fireplace but she always refused because the dough would not rise well. The only thing that people during the war had plenty of was water.

Debora usually liked the tolling of the church bells. In her little town the deacon was very good at making music with the bells. He could play a different tune for each occasion. During the war the tune was usually melancholy and sad. Debora when listening to it, always, got goose bumps and wanted to weep. The church bells played this sad military tune when the military notified some family that their soldier family member had died in the war. The bells of the church tolled for a dead soldier. After the toll of the bells everybody in the town would inquire who the dead soldier was, then, in turn, family and friends would go to the abode of the bereaved family trying to comfort and help. For three days the closest friends and family would comfort the bereaved. At times the condolences were given singing in a doleful way. While so doing they would recount the good qualities of the deceased and how much they would miss them. At the funeral everybody wore black clothes. The women would wear their hair loose. Often during the procession to the church the women would pull their hair and scratch their faces in despair. When a soldier died, the government sent a letter to the police station. The chief policemen would deliver the letter personally to the family of the deceased. Usually after the few ritual words of comfort, the letter would say that their loved one had died a hero. The mother of the deceased would chant, "Mr. Policeman, I don't want a hero; I want my son back home with me." She would sob bitterly and painfully say, "Where are you my son? Who did close your eyes? Did anyone kiss you goodbye?" The sobbing would continue. It was heart breaking. This lamentable voice could be heard for days. A dead soldier can be a hero, yes, but he is lost to his family and his country. Wars bring pain, destruction, and hardship to everybody and the most dangerous events can happen.

Debora felt that she almost killed her family because she (by accident) took home from their family store fertilizer instead of salt for her family's cooking. At that time regular salt could not be found, so 'sea salt' which was a dark crystallized salt from the sea was substituted for it. Debora was not seven years old when she went to the store to get the salt. The fertilizer and the salt were almost alike so she mistakenly brought home fertilizer instead of salt because no one had labeled either sack. Both were beside each other and she did not notice the difference. Debora, after the people left the church, was afraid to be in the church alone, but she comforted herself because she knew that soon enough the last service of the day would start and she would have company, at least for a while. After the last service, she lied down on a pew and fell asleep. Later she woke up and, since she did not know where to go, she decided to sleep in the church counting on the protection of the Virgin Mary. After fervently praying to God, she fell asleep. After a while, a soft voice gently calling her name awakened her.

It was a Friar that had woke her. He wore a black tunic with written on the left side of it the word "CHARITAS" The word 'Charitas' is a Latin word that translates in English to 'charity'. He was smiling and was telling her "child wake up and go home, nothing has happened. Everybody is OK. Your father is searching and weeping for you." Debora had been sound asleep. It took her awhile to wake up and remember where she was. Then she remembered and hearing that her father was searching and weeping for her she got up and started walking towards the door before getting out she turned her head to thank the friar but no one was there, she stopped a moment to look around the church but the friar was nowhere to be seen. Once she was out of the door, she turned her head again and someone had closed and locked the door. At once she was assailed by an inexplicable fear and she ran. She ran until she bumped in her father's arms. Her father was going towards the church searching for her as he had thought that she could have gone to church to hide.

Once safe in her father's arms she started crying desperately and between sobs she said "Dad I ran because I was scared that I did something wrong." "I know, Debora, we all know that you could not have known which of the two sacks was salt, my dear girl!", Her father, while caressing her head, told her that everybody was fine and no one would die or be injured on account of her mistake. He told her that the blame was not hers because someone should have warned her about the fertilizer and the salt looking alike and that the unlabeled sacks were beside each other. When they arrived home, everybody was trying to comfort her. Her mother while giving her a big hug presented to her a rag doll that she had made while she was waiting and praying for her safe return. While her mother hugged her tight she told her with tears in her eyes that for the love of God not to ever run away again because she had been very scared and unhappy. She thought she would never see her daughter again. Debora hugged her mother back and told her, "I will never do it again mamma, never, I promise!" Debora kissed her mother and went to play with her new rag doll.

The story of the salt and the fertilizer was never forgotten by Debora's brothers and sisters. Since then, whenever her brothers and sisters wanted to tease her, they would say to one another (most of the time in front of friends) "do you know why we are so tall?" They would answer, "Because Debora fed us fertilizer for four days during the war." All of them would laugh and at times, everyone at once would start recounting the story to her shame and embarrassment.

The Running Moon

I came from a big family. We were 14 members; my parents, 10 children, 1 grand aunt, and 1 unmarried aunt. I believe that the reason my parents had so many of us was because, Benito Mussolini, the prime minister of Italy, under the reign of the king Vittorio Emanuele III gave special prices and privileges to the 'famiglie numerose' (big families), The number of children my parents had was 11 - 4 girls and 7 boys. The first daughter died very young. If you watched the movie cheaper by the dozen you can have an idea of what was going on every day especially in the morning. My parents were merchants. They had a shop, so they would leave the house at 8 o clock in the morning to return at 9 o'clock at night. One aunt and one grand aunt stayed with us during the day but would go to their home at night after our parents came home. My mother used to get up very early in the morning to prepare us for the day ahead. When my aunts arrived in the morning both my parents would go to the store. I was born after 3 boys. Because the first girl had passed away when she was eight months old, everybody spoiled me. We were not rich but my parents managed to build a small summer house in the country. As soon as school ended my parents would put us in a (carretta) coach driven by 2 mules and take us, including the 2 aunts, to the summer house. The summer house was not very big; it had 2 large rooms and a kitchenette. Our parents would visit us on weekends. How could we manage to sleep all fourteen of us in four Large beds is beyond me. But we did, and no one ever complained. All the children, although we missed our parents, loved to go to the country during the summer vacation. We had a lot of space outside and a lot of freedom to go around the wild berry bushes to pick fresh juicy fruits and play with small animals. What we liked to do best was to capture butterflies, and scarabs. Often accompanied by one of our aunts and our dog we would go deep in the woods to pick-up mushrooms, and other eatable wild vegetables

The house was built in the lovely countryside in a place named San Demetrio. In the back of the house there was a vineyard with a lot of fruit trees strung out in a line to form the border of the vineyard. In front of the house a beautiful view could be enjoyed. It looked down the valley to the numerous towns and fields beyond. Further away the distant horizon at sundown became a belt of orange, red and pale blue colors. The birds were freely flying all around us. Quite apart from our summer house there were many villas that would be empty during the winter but became alive during the summer like our summer house did. After dusk everything became quieter. The lights of the villas and houses around lighted up and with the lights of the close and far away towns offered beautiful scenery. Every night sitting on the doorsteps of the house looking at the moon I would dream about flying to faraway places, like the birds fly. In the morning I would wake up to the continuous chirping of the cicadas, at times their monotonous chirping would be broken by a bird singing. All around was simply beautiful and peaceful. But everything would change in the morning; After washing up and having had breakfast we all had to do our chores, after that we were very busy making plans for the day ahead. Our plans concerned the way we played and what that day's enjoyment was. We were very vocal and we were always screaming and ordering one another around. The dog would do his part by barking and chasing us where ever we went. The dog's name was Rubin, it liked to run after lizards and bring them home to the horror of my aunties who were afraid of them. In truth there was never a dull moment.

There is an ancient saying that goes "Children have a guardian angel watching over them." However, for what could have happened and did not happen, God must have sent an army of angels to watch over us. My brothers liked to play the Indians at war with Tom Mix a hero of the past, who was, always fighting the Indians. When playing the Indians my brothers would dress and act like Indians at war. They would pluck feathers from our chickens, sow them on a ribbon and then put them around their heads, strip themselves from the waist up, build a drum using a cloth tied by stretched and stripped wet tree branches around a cooking pan to make the tom-tom sound. Then they would flip a coin to find the renegade who would be tied to a tree, I never participated in this kind of play, then, they would proceed to chanting and screaming running around the tree to the rhythm of the drum. Until the chief, sitting bull, would order the punishment for the renegade. The punishment was to take one of us around the house on his back behaving like a horse. Another favorite play scene was; to free a princess in bondage. The princess was our two year old little sister Doretta. Our two aunts would hold her pretending to be guards; my aunts did not have the choice to refuse to participate in the play for two reasons. The liberators when not seen would throw stones and dirt in the house and our aunties would never know who had done it. Secondly, my aunts were afraid that our little sister would be in danger. My little sister would stay put as long as she could eat chocolates provided by our aunts. I also believe that she found all the uproar amusing. My brothers would find many other kinds of dangerous plays. Sometimes they played at hunting the wolves that occasionally would wander down from the high mountains. We would not wear shoes, during the summer when close to the house. We never wore shoes, when playing in front of the house and on the grass, when playing to catch the wolves. We would make ourselves rifles made of wood branches with a rope tied at both ends of the branch. The youngest of the brothers would put a hood on his head to be the wolf. He would hide and the wolf hunters would find him and shoot him by throwing at him an empty food can as a bullet.

Our parents never knew how dangerously we were playing. No one had courage to tell them how dangerously we played because everyone was too tired by the time they would finally arrive on Saturday night. On Sunday no one liked to upset our parents. We had so little time together. We all stayed around them asking questions and telling them the good stories and the good happenings of the week. After the family attended church and had lunch we would stay home until they left for the store in the city using a coach that harnessed mules pulled. We would follow them in a procession and singing our promises to them. "Mom and dad, we will be good. We promise that we will be very good!" We sang for about a quarter of a mile. When the road turned, we always were happy to see our parents smile while they waived their hands good bye.

I was a quite child seemingly to be always in thought. I liked the sounds of the night and I watched the moon for hours while dreaming of touching it. My dreams about the moon went as far as taking the moon, like a ball, home to play with my brothers and sisters. It didn't seem to be hard it was so close. Sometimes, I could see a larger white moon in the late afternoon. It looked like it was so close that I could pick it out of the air. On one of those days, I decided that I should visit the Moon. If possible, I wanted to take it and bring it with me home to see my family. Usually my playing occurred in the afternoon. We were busy in the morning because all of us had chores to do. Therefore, on an afternoon when all were busy playing, I started to walk in direction of the Moon barefooted as I said before when we were in the country we often did not wear shoes. I walked and walked, all the time feeling that I was getting closer and closer to the moon. I would bet with myself that the moon was as far as one hundred feet, I would then walk faster counting the one hundred steps, but the moon had walked further away. The sun was no longer so hot and was disappearing. It was swallowed quickly by the horizon. Dusk was approaching. The Moon was more brilliant, larger, and it seemed to be closer to me. I was very tired; my feet were hurting and bleeding. I could no longer hear the chirping of the birds, instead I was hearing swishing sounds. There were fewer birds flying in the sky. I began to be worried. The sky was filling with clouds. How if it rains? I thought I am all alone here without an umbrella. Then, while I was thinking, the moon started moving all at once first towards me, then away from me. I extended both my arms trying desperately to catch it but it started running faster and faster. I ran after it for a while it didn't seem to slow down at all. Very tired and in pain I sat down on the ground crying, feeling dejected and defeated. It was getting darker and darker and I was very scared. I knew that there were wolves around so each innocuous sound terrified me. I really thought I was going to be eaten by wolves.

I began to pray to God to help me. I cried and called to my mother. Then as if a miracle had happened, I began to hear, from far away, a multitude of voices calling my name. Immediately I felt safe and started to feel better. I, also, realized that it was wrong of me to go so far away from home alone without telling anybody. So, I was a little afraid of being punished when I returned home. Nevertheless, nothing could compare with the sense of joy and safety I felt when I heard the voices of the many people in my family. My feet were bleeding and very painful I could not get up to meet them, by then was quite dark and since my family was searching for me, I waited for them to come closer. As they got close enough, I answered back. Within moments I was encircled by my family who were very happy to see me! Everybody was kissing me, hugging me, and wanting to know how I was. Unfortunately all this mirth did not last very long, and inquiring irate faces began to appear. All were asking the same questions at the same time. "What are you doing here?" "Why did you come here?" I started to cry very loudly to release my tension and to make an exaggerated expression of distress to make my punishment less severe. I knew that I would be punished for what I had done. I calmed down a bit but I was still incapable of answering anybody's questions.

When my grandaunt panting and scared out of her wits arrived, she asked "What happened girl? You better explain! I have never been so scared and worried for you in my life." "Oh aunty," I answered while continuing to weep "I just came to visit and catch the moon, but it ran away before I could even touch it." Complete silence followed my answer. For a moment the many sounds of the forest could be heard again. Everyone was now speechless, but then everybody began to laugh loudly and heartily. My older brother took me in his arms and, while he was carrying me home, said to me: "The Moon did not run, you stupid girl. The Moon does not run. The clouds moved over the Moon and it seemed to you that the moon was running under the clouds. Don't ever do anything like that again or you will get in serious trouble." Hugging him tight, I screamed, "I won't, I promise not to go out alone ever again" The day after I will not tell you what my punishment was for the Moon adventure but I am sure you can guess. The next day my brothers were very busy, teaching a lesson to the renegade squaw who went on foot to catch the moon.

Maurice, My Never Forgotten Scary Friend

*M*aurice and I were not really friends in the true sense of the word. He lived nearby our store and I was always scared when I saw him. He was a beggar. He hardly ever spoke to anybody. He never asked for money, food, or anything else that he might have wanted. When he needed help he would stand at any corner of a street looking at his swollen red hands. People were used to his silent presence and, when helping him, they did not expect thanks or any other word from him. Many people thought that he was mute. Sometimes he would come to our store and would stand close to the entrance waiting for help from the people that came into our store to shop. At other times he would sit down on the corner of the first step of the shop door, just leaving enough space for shoppers to enter or exit until my mother would give him a penny or something to eat. I was very young then and even today after sixty years I cannot explain my fascination with him. When I saw him go home, I would make sure that his pockets were full with food to eat. During the cold winter if I saw him with broken shoes held together with pieces of old lace of cloth or without shoes at all I would run to my mother and I would then beg her to give to Maurice an old pair of my father's shoes. My mother, always, acquiesced to my request but bade me to stay away from Maurice, because he did not like to be fussed around and that I was too young to go following him. Maurice was a very poor man. He was of medium height, plump, clothed in rags, and dirty; he wore a cap and kept one hand clasped on top of the other. He, also, came to beg in front of the school often. When the school let out, the children would wait until he left, then they followed him screamed at him, laughed at him, and called him names. He would be patient for a while, but then he would scream with an incredible thunderous voice at all of us. At which point we would run away. We were not really afraid of him. In fact, after having run away, because the teachers left the school at day's end, some children would come back again to be more vocal and vicious. One day some children after the usual screams and verbal insults threw stones at him. He tried to protect himself with his hands without saying a word. On that day, fortunately, the teachers came out to disperse us. Many teachers gave to him money. The next day the teachers reprimanded and punished all of us. They forbade us to ever again scream, make fun or in any way harass Maurice. Above all, they told us that if anyone threw a stone at Maurice again, the school would suspend any offender. The school sent a letter to our parents informing them of what had happened and the sanction that would follow if they did not make sure that their children stopped badgering Maurice. The school board was very serious about the matter. I had never thrown any stones at him, but I did, to my own shame, unite with the other children in yelling at him. Looking back at our yelling, I often wonder why we were so cruel. Why do most of us have the tendency to oppress, persecute, and ridicule the weak? He was just standing there looking at us and expecting some charity. Every time that we were malicious to Maurice, I would feel very guilty, after that I would promise to myself I would not repeat my behavior again. Unfortunately, I forgot, or my peers influenced me. Anyway, the parents read the letters sent to them by the school regarding the stoning of Maurice. They assured the school board that they had spoken to their children and they had reprimanded us. They assured the school that their child would never do something so heinous and cruel again. To the best of my knowledge it never did. Nevertheless, they grounded me for a week.

When Maurice did not come to our store, my mother would send me to his place to bring him some food. I would gladly go, also, because I was curious to see the inside of his place. Once there, on tip toes, I would try to enter. Nevertheless, Maurice would explosively chase me from the door while he whispered incomprehensible words. He would pretend to catch me while I ran away.

I would run away, occasionally jerking my head back to see if he was following me. One time, I tried to enter his place again when he was sleeping. While tiptoeing past the door, I entered with my heart thumping furiously. As my eyes adjusted to the light, I stood speechless, suddenly realizing with horror that his place was only about 2 meters long and less than 1 meter wide. He did not have a chair or a table but 2 large flat stones that served as both. The only other thing in his place was a very dirty blanket on, what seemed to me, a cobblestone floor. It was winter and the left side of the place was filled with ashes. A last piece of black coal was still burning in the ashes. The ceiling and the walls were black as there was nowhere the smoke could escape except to go out through the front door. The place was getting cold, so much so, that I was shaking. All at once, I wanted to cry and to run, but before I could do anything, I saw Maurice standing in front me, calmly looking at me, he did not do or say anything, he just kept looking at me. Then he looked at the door, I got the message and I started to run but as I started to run, I saw a flicker of a smile on his face. After this encounter, I never saw Maurice's face again. I think that my demeanor and look on my face must have humiliated him because when I went to bring food to him again, the person next door told me to leave the food in front of the door. My mother did not send me there again; my younger brother took my job.

I had been touched too deeply by Maurice's living conditions. I started asking around the school and marketplace about Maurice and his brother Sebastian. Sebastian made his living working for the church of the Virgin of Carmel. Sebastian would carry a wooden box with the image of the Virgin Mary painted on it. He would go all over our little town chanting, "Please, good people help the church in honor of our Lady of the Carmel and she in thankfulness will help you too." Sebastian would try to help Maurice but he could barely feed and clothe himself. This was happening in 1946, too close to the end of World War II for comfort. Most of us did not have enough of the basic necessities of life; like food, clothes, and soap. I remember that I cried every morning because I had to wear a dress made of an old military blanket and a pair of shoes three sizes bigger then my feet. I did my investigation regarding Maurice and Sebastian. What I found out was very disconcerting. It explained to certain extent why Maurice behaved the way he did.

Maurice and Sebastian were the children of the richest landlord of the county, Don Jacinto Martelli. He came from a very rich family, so much so that his mother and father owned, among many other extravagant precious things, a sculpture of one large hen with 12 chicks that was made of heavy gold. Maurice's father was a very good looking man; he dressed elegantly, had many servants and was a spendthrift. He liked beautiful women, have rich parties. He also was addicted to gambling. A few years after the death of his parents, Maurice's father Don Jacinto Martelli had spent three quarters of his inheritance. His wife, lady Constanza was the daughter of a count; she used to live in splendor, and did not pay much attention to the management of the household. She was a beautiful woman who liked to dress well, wear precious jewels. Travel in new and elegant carriages to visit her relatives very often. Her relatives lived in the next county of Cartoon, and she would leave her house uncontrolled in the hands of her servants. The land had been sold parcel by parcel, as the money was needed. Most of the expensive jewels of lady Constanza had been sold too. At one point they found themselves in debts with almost all their suppliers to the point that they could not feed themselves. The servants left taking all they could as payment for their rendered services.

It was a total disaster in the end, don Jacinto with the hope of winning and the intention of saving himself and his family, gambled away all the rest of his inheritance. He lost everything. After being evicted from his Family's house he shot himself. His wife and 4 children were left with nothing but desperation. Distant relatives took the wife and two girls to their far away home, but no one wanted the two very young boys. In the end, both boys found the street was their home and garbage was their food and supplies.

The boys were too young to understand; they cried and asked people for help. Although everybody realized that the children were innocent, the people of the town were not very sympathetic towards the children. Nevertheless, some people helped the two children when they could. When they did not have anything to eat, they ate garbage and slept behind doors. During the very cold winter days in that part of the country, they would try to sleep in barns, or wherever they could find a warm place. Sebastian was the older of the two brothers, and he tried to cope with their misfortune as much as he could. He would do odd small jobs, he could read and write and sometimes people would ask him to read or write a letter for food or small change. Maurice, instead, would scream and desperately demand to be taken to his mother and father. During the winter, especially at night, Maurice's screams would wake people up. Those people would then call the police who, in turn, would put the two unfortunate boys into a warm jail cell. Perhaps they put them in jail because it was so cold outside, but they let them out at dawn. After a while, the church intervened because of the continuous asking of so many people. The church fed them and provided shelter for them at night. Maurice stopped crying, but started talking less and less as he got older. He never went to school, he never played with other children, he never went to church, and he just retreated into a world of his own. He never emerged from that isolated world. How very sad. Sebastian kept his job with the church, and as he grew up he assumed more responsibilities with the church and both boys benefited from it. Nevertheless, the church did very little for poor Maurice.

The stress and trauma for the loss of his family destroyed a young life that may have been a great one. It is speculation, I know, but I cannot stop asking myself why no one would help these two unhappy children? Maybe their parents had been rich and abusive towards the people of the town? This is also speculation, I will never know. What I know is that I will never be able to forget Maurice; but why is he so memorable to me? He was not related to me or close to my family. It was, perhaps, the stress of seeing a human being living in a subhuman condition and the people, the church, and the government not saving him. My heart tells me that there must be a much deeper reason, but while I cannot think of what it can be, I send prayers to God for poor unlucky Maurice.

A Matter of Egotism

The room was long and narrow. On the left, near the entrance door, stood an altar; on the altar a statue of the Virgin Mary stood in prayer. The altar was surrounded with flowers and lit candles. The room was full of people reciting the holy Rosary. All these prayers were to help the health of my older Brother Antonino who was in the hospital dying of meningitis. All at once, there was silence in the room; my father had come to tell us that Antonino, my dear brother, had died. After the sorrowful announcement my father requested that the altar, the flowers, and the candles be taken away because my mother was on her way home, from the hospital. She was in a poor emotional state. She could not believe that the first flower of her life as she called him was no more. My mother never recovered from the death of my brother. She completely lost it. Both my parents believed that education was the most important part of anybody's life. All of their 10 children at that time were going to school. In my little town there was no university, so two of the eldest children were studying in Sicily, Antonino studied in Palermo and Joseph studied in Messina. The others studied in less expensive schools.

Antonino got sick. He had continuous headaches and severe sore knees. He had just discussed and passed his final oral examination for his doctorate in law. In less than a week he had to be rushed to the hospital. The doctors diagnosed him with meningitis - both cerebral and spinal meningitis. The best doctors of the hospital got involved to fight his disease with no avail. We had medical specialists come all the way from Rome, but no one could save my brother; and, in less than a week, he died.

It was a terrible blow. My family went from rich and happy to very unhappy and on its way to Bankruptcy in less than a year. My brother Joseph, after 4 years of medical studies, decided that he did not care to become an MD anymore because medicine had failed his brother. Joseph thought that if a team of the best doctors in the best hospital of Catanzaro, the capital of Calabria, could not save Antonino, our brother, then he no longer believed he could be a doctor or save anybody. But each one in my family was so shocked and grief stricken that none of us could function. After all, my brother began complaining of a pain in his neck, which spread to his head and to his knees just a week before his death. At that time, we started a long fall into bankruptcy. The death of my brother came so devastatingly fast and because my parents had heavily borrowed money to pay for our education, we were financially at risk. After his death, all our creditors wanted their money back and fast too. I had always thought that I loved my brother the most, and could not survive his death, but I became the strongest of my family. My second brother Francesco was a Sergeant with the police. The Carabinieri (National Police) stationed him at Rovigo in northern Italy. With Francesco's help, Joseph joined the University of Padova to become a lawyer while working part-time as a legal clerk. All the other children managed to complete that year's study and then had to stop going to private colleges and transfer to public schools. A year after my brother's death our finances were almost depleted and our family's lenders, especially the banks and relatives wanted their monies almost immediately. Something had to be done. I asked for help to my Aunt Domenica that at the time was visiting her daughter Dorothy who was teaching the children of the American soldiers stationed at Aviano Italy.

My Bostonian Aunt invited me to visit her while she was visiting her daughter in Aviano, Italy. Aviano is in the North Italy between Venice and Padova. I stayed with my aunt and her daughter one month, and then I went to visit my brother Joseph in Padova. Joseph's girlfriend, Luciana, was studying fashion design. Since I had told her that I was looking for a job, she told me that her school was looking for teachers. I had previously taken a yearlong fashion design course in Rome that I passed, but because my school was a private college, even though I was qualified, I had to take another fashion design course to become a fashion design teacher with this school. I passed the final exam and the school hired me immediately.

The school offered me the choice to teach in Padova or Milano. I chose Milano. I followed my brother Joseph's advice because Milano was a very industrialized and rich city, and it was possible for all our family members to find jobs there. Here, in the civilized, rich, industrialized city of Varese, which was forty km. from Milano in the same province of Varesotto, I experienced the cruelty and despair of discrimination. Nineteen provinces make up Italy. Each province differs in its individual culture. Each province speaks a different dialect with a different accent, has different way of cooking, a different mental outlook with a different way to see and to judge situations and behavior, but I have to say that we all are united by the Italian Language.

Between north and south Italy, at the time, there was a barrier of distrust and arrogance, now it is not as bad. In the north, the people derogatorily call the people of the south "Terroni", which means a bunch of ignorant and, at times, violent peasants. I have a lot of sympathy and feelings for the emigrants of all nations and creeds because I know the frustration and impotence of being treated and addressed like a half human. I cannot make a complete parallel with our Mexican illegal immigrants because no matter what happened, I could not be deported. But other than that I have immensely suffered at the hands of the bigots and egotistical people that are everywhere in the world. My family had reached a point where we no longer could stay in town; we closed our shop, we sold the house. I found myself in urgent need of finding an apartment or house, so I started to search for one in my spare time. I went to agencies and searched in the newspaper, but I could not find one. The agencies did not seem to have any houses or apartments available at any moment that I asked for one. The people that I called would pause a moment to recognize my accent when they answered the phone, then I would hear, "le sa ghe a terrona", which means 'she is a terrona' at which point they would say that the place was no longer available or would just hang up. Every day after hearing this statement, so many times I began to weep and pray for better luck tomorrow. While this was happening I was assigned to teach in the town of Tecedre in a Franciscan convent.

The Mother Superior and the sisters were wonderful; they were very attentive to my needs and always ready to help. In this convent I found an angel in sister Placida, she was small, neat, and always smiling. She always asked me how I was, one day after class when she asked me how things were going, I could not help myself and began to weep and told her everything. She got both my hands in hers and told me, "Please signorina Teresa" (she had, since the beginning, refused to call me by just my name) "do not weep, we will help you if we can, to begin with we all will pray for you tonight, but, please, don't weep!" The next day with the permission and help of the mother superior she had found, for me, a cheaper place to stay. For a very small price I was already eating at the convent. A few days later sister Placida ran towards me after class smiling, "I have good news; I have good news for you, Miss. God forgive me for what I have done, come with me", then she whispered, "the mother superior knows," then she proceeded to tell me, "there is in the office a Mr. Varatti who has a small apartment for rent, I have told him that you are French teacher and he has agreed to meet you." I felt hopeful so I ran with her. Mr. Varatti seemed a nice gentleman. We shook hands and wrote the contract; he told me that since the mother superior and sister Placida had vouched for me he did not need any other reference. After I paid him, Sister Placida said, "Mr. Varatti, will you please forgive me. I have sinned to-wards God and you. Please do forgive me." Sister Placida with her hands in the pose of praying was imploring him for forgiveness. He, completely taken aback, said, "Yes, yes, sister Placida for whatever it is I forgive you." Sister Placida told him, "Mr. Varatti, Miss Teresa is not French; she is Calabrese, a terrona." He was speechless for a moment then he screamed, "You tricked me, sister Placida. You tricked me!" The sister replied, "I did it for God's love. You know, no one wants to rent a place to her because she is a terrona, Terroni are children of God too. Mr. Varatti looked at me and said, "You seem honest enough and clean enough to treat my place well," then he turned his head to talk with sister Placida. He said, "It is OK, Sister Placida. You always manage to win your battles." Then he gave me the apartment keys and his card and left. After a year, we moved from his apartment to a bigger place. When I went to his office to return the keys, he took my hands in his and said, "Please do me the honor to have a cup of coffee with me." I accepted gladly. He thanked me for having improved his house while using it. He told me that he would never discriminate against the people of the south again. Then he asked me to please call him if we needed help." We shook hands and departed as the best of friends.

Similar situations, I think, happen to our Mexican immigrants here as well. How can we reconcile our sense of justice with exploitation of the poor and un-wary immigrants? I am sure that if we thought about it when we enjoy eating our juicy fruit and lush vegetables, our conscience would nag us. Maybe, if in our minds, we would picture the illegal immigrants, bending down to pick the fruits and vegetables for pennies, we would feel uneasy! But regardless we continue to put up fences with guards knowing that fences will not stop the exodus but cause death and despair. Fences cannot stop people in need, especially when they are hungry. Guards can-not avoid shedding blood while trying to stop hungry people from entering the country's workforce. So long as there are available jobs that Americans will not fill, the injury and death of immigrants will not appease our conscience. Just the same, immigrants, in general, are like addicts. Their addiction cannot be stopped. Their addiction is not an unfortunate but lethal vice. The immigrants are addicted to food, life, and doing the best they can for their children. The lure of a better life is much greater than the knowledge of danger. Also, there is the hope of not being caught. They try to enter America with God's help. Let us picture in our minds a family of 4, 2 parents with 2 children, these parents cannot feed or clothe their children adequately. They have no education and no job, as things go, they cannot even dream of a better future, remember Elian Gonzales' mother? She lost her life trying to come to America for a better future for herself and her son. She never made it to the USA, only her son did. The price for the fences and guards is staggering; we are talking of billions of dollars. Mexico's rigid class based society has laws that throw many people of its middle and low classes, "mainly poor" people, at our borders. We cannot become guards and build fences controlling our population and their population. This is what destroyed Roman Civilization long ago. We are a people who give equal opportunity and treatment under the law to all. As we say on our money, "IN GOD WE TRUST". It is enshrined in our declaration of independence and constitution. To allow discriminatory treatment of workers living here induces a class based society of inhuman laws. It will destroy us just like it destroyed Rome. We can only allow anyone who is here the same rights and responsibilities as all of us. Work passes and illegal immigrant deportation will not solve any of our problems. If anyone chooses to live here and speaks the English language, then they should have the right to learn our history and government and become American citizens. Our government should only deport violent criminals. It is easy for government agents to discriminate against immigrants by accusing them of immigration crimes or other nonviolent crimes designed to fix someone into a lower class life.

Trepido

*J*anet Pellegrini would remember the year 1950 for all her life. During 1950, at the age of fifteen, she went to visit Italy for the first time with her father. She had heard so much about the beauty of this fantastic country that she could not wait to board a plane and finally go and see it. Janet had been preparing her suitcase for a week on the last day she was in a frenzy. Her room was in chaos. The place looked like a junkyard with dresses, books, coats, pantyhose, overturned chairs, and a hundred other things scattered all over the place. Each time that she checked her suitcase to see if anything was missing, she found a host of missing things that she would need. She was at her wits end, so she ran crying to her mother for help. When Mrs. Carole Pellegrini entered the room, looked at her daughter, then after being speechless for a moment, she said, "Child, what is this? Calm down! Everything is going to be OK. I will help you pack. You have put in this suitcase enough clothes and stuff to stay for at least a two Month vacation, but you will stay there only three weeks." She took her daughter in her arms, kissed her on the head, then she said, "C'mon honey, let's pack your suitcase together." She placed the suitcase over the bed, and then she started refilling it by selecting each item. When she had finished packing what her daughter needed, the suitcase was three quarters full. Now her daughter, Janet, put a book or two, a magazine and her toiletry bag stuff in the suitcase. She found that she was all done. Janet had stopped crying. Now, she actually smiled, thanked, and hugged her mother, and then she happily ran out to get some more things. Mrs. Carole Pellegrini was a comely woman, she was a little overweight, and she had green eyes and blond hair that she wore in a bun at the back of her head. She had eleven children but her first child, a little girl that died when she was 8 months old, had changed her greatly. She could not deny any of her children anything without thinking of how suddenly and fast her first baby had died. She always championed her children's goals and needs before her own. She had a big heart, and she would do anything she could to help people. She was a very smart woman who was a bookkeeper in her husband's business. She took care of her family and the business with the help of an unmarried sister and her eldest daughter, Janet. Mr. Pat Pellegrini had relatives living in the Italian region of Calabria. They lived in the mountains in the village of Trepidó.

After visiting Rome, Venice, and Florence, Janet and her father would board another plane for Crotone, the capital of Calabria and then they would continue their trip in a coach carried by horses up to the mountains of La Sila to Trepidó. Janet was very happy. The three beautiful cities she had seen enchanted her. Roma simply delighted her, especially the big plaza of Vatican City; the splendor of Saint Peter's Church, the Bernini Colonnade, Fountain of Trevi, and the Coliseum captivated both her mind and her thoughts. How could, such architectural jewels have been built without mechanization and electricity? It was a mystery to her. Images of slaves being beaten and starved crowded her mind around the Trevi Fountain, Colonnade, and the Coliseum, but medieval and renaissance masons had built Saint Peter's and the Vatican as a monument to their beliefs. However, she thought that none their suffering had not been in vain because people admired their work even now, after so many years. She acknowledged their sacrifices and sent her thoughts of love to those who created such beauty.

Florence for her was the epitome of beauty imagination and creativity. Florence is a witness to the glory and magnificence, of true art, splendor and the will to ascend to highest altitudes of the human spirit. The art of the past artists was simply sublime to her. Venice was a wonder to her, she had heard of the magnificent city that ran into the sea, but she could not believe that it could be true until she saw it. It was a city in the sea, how splendid and unbelievable it was. I thought that I was living in a dream.

Piazza San Marco was so rich, so beautiful, and so crowded with tourists. Birds flew in the air above and flocked to the square below where tourists fed them bread. Spinning around watching the birds made Janet's head spin to the point that she thought that she was seasick. Her father was talking to her, but she could not hear anything he said. When she felt better, she found herself in a gondola. The gondola carved of wood was long and narrow. On the wood outside there were designs of flowers and mermaids (sirens). Wanting to make sure that what she was living was true and not a dream, she turned towards the side of the gondola and touched the water to make sure that she was not dreaming. She almost fell into the canal. Her father caught her and said, "Take it easy girl. Your experiences here are true, and there is no danger, besides I am with you. I will never let anything happen to you." The gondolier gave her a piece of chocolate while saying in Italian, "Signorina, (young girl) there is no danger we are in the sea but it is like we were on terra firma. Smile! Smile! Life is beautiful. Look how many people are around us, but nobody is afraid." Janet calmed down as her father translated the gondolier's words. She started looking around and seeing so many happy people. She felt very happy, but she also felt foolish and inadequate. It was in the afternoon and she was very hungry. Her father saw a small restaurant, so they went to the trattoria (small pasta restaurant) where the specialty of the day was pasta al forno, and they found it was delicious, she never thought that pasta al forno, could taste so good. To show to her father that she wasn't afraid anymore she asked him to take her to the sea to have another ride in the gondola. This time she was prepared and enjoyed the ride immensely. It was time now to go to the mountains to visit Janet's relatives in the village of Trepidó.

The road up the hill to Trepidó was narrow and uneven. At times, the coach would hit a stone and their seat would jump up and down. The surprise jostling would relieve the monotony of the journey. A young man by the name of Joe was traveling with them to Trepidó. Joe was the son of a friend of Mr. Pellegrini's family who served as a guide to the mountains and to the Pellegrini family in Trepidó. Joe was tall; he had black eyes and black wavy hair. His long exposure to the sun tanned his brownish skin. He had strong white teeth and a beautiful smile that completely dominated his face, when he smiled he looked very handsome. Janet liked him, but she felt annoyed by the fact that he kept his knee against her leg. She felt really uneasy and mad at herself because she didn't have the courage to tell him to move over. She realized, though, that there was not much space between them. In fact, only one bench went from one side to the other side of the coach. There was barely enough space for three people, still he didn't have to touch her knee. Joe was very knowledgeable about the country side and tried to explain and describe to them all that was interesting and new about the history of the place and the changes that progress had slowly brought. As they climbed higher and higher the view of their surroundings changed. On the right side there were bushes and wild flowers. Looking higher up the hill sheep, cows, and sometimes, horses grazed under the care of the people who tended the animals. The sheep had bells on their necks and when the sheep jumped from one bush to another one, the bells jingled. They heard and enjoyed the sweet sound of the bells. Sometimes a large black dog would stop briefly to look at them while the dog minded the sheep. From the left side the breathtaking view continued to change. Below the road, hundreds of trees big and small fought for space, while farther away as the valley opened up toward the horizon small cities, villages, and towns showed many red clay tile roofs irradiated by the sun. The scene created a picture of light and color. Looking farther away, the sky met the sea in the distance. It looked like an oasis populated by distant doves. Little barges, looking like toys, moved in the sea far away. Above the sea, the sky was very blue and small white ever-changing scattered clouds about moved over the sky.

Joe, always attached to Janet's knee, would tell her "Janet look ahead of you. Look how tall the trees are here." She would look and could not help enchanting herself with the view. She wanted to scream that the scene of the slender tall trees was very beautiful. Birds flew around chirping at each other. It seemed they tried to catch one another. Janet had never seen such a beauty and was truly enchanted. A few times, they had to stop because another coach would pass them on the hill. The road was so narrow that when they passed each other they almost touched. When that occurred, Janet would turn to her father for protection. As they continued climbing, the plateau seemed enlarged and the trees seemed taller and larger in the distance. During our ride, we passed a few cottages here and there. Then the sound of running water surprised her because she did not expect it. Janet asked Joe, "Is this sound a river running around here?" Joe replied, "Yes, it is the river Trepidó. It is a large river and we can catch the biggest and most delicious trout here in the river." Finally, they arrived at a large flat area, the river was quite large, the water was clean, and it hurried down the valley rippling loudly. All around there were tall trees and large bushes. Some bushes had yellow flowers, while other bushes had large leaves and pink and white flowers. Birds flew from bush to bush singing lovely songs; it seemed that they chased each other. All around everything was harmonious and festive. Janet's father and Joe stopped to fish for trout while she looked with fascination at the blue sky and faraway horizon. The river had so many trout that was easy to catch them. Janet had never seen a fish die before, so she was shocked and bewildered by their twisting in pain, and then they lay still with their open mouth. Janet's father had already cleaned some of the trout and cooked them. A delicious smell assailed her nostrils. She had not eaten since the morning, so she ran towards the cooking fish and the fire to eat while forgetting the trout's dying agony. Janet's father had noticed her dismay and, while presenting her with a dish of delicious smelling trout, he put his right arm around her shoulder and said, "Janet don't feel so hurt. This is how things are, God made the fish for us to eat, even Jesus gave fishes to eat to his hungry followers. Be happy, child. Be happy. I don't know if we will ever have another beautiful day like today. To tell the truth Janet, I had forgotten all about our supper dying." She hugged her father and began to eat voraciously. Near where we ate, there was a fountain. The water seemed to come from the root of a tree and flowed on a deep long brown tile. Water does' not have flavor but, believe me, that this water tasted divine.

It was time to resume their journey to their relative's house a couple of miles ahead from the river. Under a fresh breeze they continued their trip. No matter in which direction they looked the panorama all around was enchanting. Far away, the tallest trees seemed to touch the sky and the ever moving clouds seemed to jump from one tree to another, then like a miracle a large blue lake appeared in the next large plateau. Small canoes containing two or three people were running from one side to the other side of the lake, while the people in the canoes sang and enjoyed themselves. In a large sandy space there were a lot of people, in bathing suits, enjoying the breeze and the sun. Janet asked her father if they could rent a canoe and go around the lake. An old man hearing her request came to them and offered his canoe at a discounted prize. Her father looked at her and seeing that she was so happy said yes.

They went in the lake and started going all around it at times they joined the other canoers singing love songs. Janet was so happy she wanted to stay there forever, but her father reminded her that their relatives were waiting for them and that they had to go. They left that little corner of paradise and resumed their trip. They finally they arrived to their destination and Janet was plunged in another kind of rural beauty and wonder.

Their relatives lived in a large house made of long tree logs, it was very big and the porch was gabled. There were several pots with flowers on the porch. Chickens roamed around the yard and chirped. Goats, sheep and cows populated the area that was closer to the house. On the back of the house in a fenced area there were three horses, two males and one female. The female had a star on the top of her head and was called Stella. Stella means star in Italian. Janet got in the saddle and rode Stella with her father at her side. She liked to ride Stella a lot. After resting a while, Janet got to look around for fresh eggs, she found many and she was so happy and proud of her find, then she milked the cow and the goats. Her relatives were still relatively young; they were in their mid forties, Uncle Michele was 46 years old aunty Clara was 42. They had 4 children 3 boys and 1 girl, Giovanni, Giacomo, Saverio and Matilda. They were born three years apart; they were still going to school. The boys were tall and good-looking. The girl was small but was a true beauty. Her hair was black wavy and very long. They all showed great affection towards them and seemed truly happy to have them. They all studied English because all the children, especially the boys, wanted to come and visit us in America. Matilda asked Janet if she had a prayer book. She said, "Yes." She asked Janet, "could I see it for a minute." when she gave it to her, she opened it in the middle, picked a camellia from a bush, and put it in the book. She returned it to Janet and told her, "Dear Janet, keep this to remember me. Every time you hold it, you will think of me." Janet was so touched that she hugged and kissed her. They spent a wonderful afternoon together. They begged them to stay longer at least until tomorrow, but they could not because they had to catch a plane the next day. They had a lot to do and see still.

Therefore, we departed. We promised to return but we never did return. Janet, after so many years, still dreamed of the area of La Sila and Trepidó. During our journey back, Joe attached his knee to Janet's leg again but she didn't mind any more. She ended up liking him and when they returned to Crotone, they separated. She was sad and for a while missed him. Had she fallen in love with him? Maybe, I definitely think that he had fallen in love with me because he tried to get in touch by mail. However, they never saw one another again. Sometimes she wondered how her life would have turned out if she had been friendlier with him and really loved him. Janet still remembers his big black eyes, his curly black hair, and his beautiful smile. One thing is sure; after so many years, Janet found herself thinking about him with a sense of loss. Janet will never be able to forget her beautiful enchanting trip to Italy and especially to La Sila and Trepidó.

Leaving My Country
and My Home

*T*he old house was a two story house. On the first floor, there was a large kitchen, a larger dining room, and a very elegant living room. Proceeding to the second floor, you had to climb two sets of stairs to reach a large and short hall. On each wall of the hall there was a door, each one was the entrance to a big bed room with wood floors. Each room had a large window where the sun shone all day long. After previously living in two medium sized rooms this house seemed a mansion to Laura, but what she liked the most was the front main entrance door to the house; it was large and elegant, although it was a little old.

On the ceiling before a short stairway, there were pictures of beautiful ladies dressed with flowers and garlands that Laura loved to admire, when she entered and when she left the house. On the other side of the house there was a small garden that we accessed through the kitchen door. In the yard amongst the flowers and well-cared green bushes, there was a table where on weekends the whole family played all kinds of games. Towards the center of the yard there was a large Hachiya persimmon tree. Laura liked persimmons and every year, when in season she enjoyed picking and eating them. She had a clear memory of her dear mother sitting on a short chair under the shadow of the tree when she ate persimmons. Laura's mother was always busy, either knitting or crocheting. Laura loved looking at her or listening to her at night recounting the day's happenings or news. Her mother had always been a workaholic. Laura always worked out of the house doing one thing or another. Her parents were sickly and Laura was the oldest of their daughters still living at home. She took care of almost everything. Of late personal things were not going well for her. After about fifteen years of refusing to meet or date anyone, Laura tired of people telling her that she was getting old and becoming a spinster. She started looking at men with the intention of finding a husband. Believe me, it was a disaster! After so many years of refusing to look at men with matrimonial intentions, she was incapable of feeling love or feeling someone loved her. She fell in love a few times, but always with the wrong guy. To tell the truth, she did not think that she really fell in love with any one of her dates. Because all her younger siblings were either married or engaged, she felt alone and left out. Only because Laura felt alone, she acquiesced to the will of her parents to get married, but every time she thought she had fallen in love, she discovered that she was not in love at all. Actually, the whole thing annoyed and upset Laura. Things got so bad that she was at the point of weeping. When things didn't work out, the suitors dumped her. After a week or so, she was happy that things had not worked out. Her father did not like what happened and pushed her to choose someone and marry him. The idea that he could have a spinster as a daughter drove him crazy. Laura did not even remember how she met the last man she dated and thought that she might love. Today she knows for sure that she did not love him, but she was lonely and tired of all the fights at home. She invited him to come home to meet her family. Her father hated him the first moment he set his eyes on him, but everybody else tried their best to be agreeable to him. His name was Percival; he was tall and thin. He seldom smiled and most of all was a pompous egotist. He was a professor of literature; he had black wavy hair and black eyes. He wore eyeglasses and darkish suits. Laura was a teacher for special students and she believed Percival didn't think she was on the same level as he was. He thought he had a great future, but he, above all, wanted to marry money and neither Laura nor her family had any. She was beautiful, but she was too old for a Don Giovanni like him because she had reached the point where she really wanted to get married. Even though she did not like or love him, she tried to get close to him. After a while, she believed that she developed some affection for him. Evidently, she tried too hard. Laura liked being with him, but she always felt that there was something missing. After agreeing that they would get married and look for a place, one afternoon he telephoned her. He suddenly told Laura that they could not marry because he didn't love her anymore. He shocked her so much that she did not answer. He hung up when the line remained silent. The call completely devastated Laura. She didn't feel any pain for losing him, but the call disappointed and hurt her because she could not believe that something like that could happen to someone who had the interest of so many men. Laura did not want her mother who was at home to see her and ask her questions, so she jumped on her bike and drove around the town for hours. When she came back home her father was furious, Percival after talking to her had called her brother Jessie to inform him of the telephone call and of his intentions. Jessie called her father. Because her father had wanted him thrown out of the house and none of the family listened to him, Percival's actions vindicated his opinion. He made sure that none of the family had anything to do with Percival. Afterwards, things were ugly between Laura and her father, to the point that she told all her family that she would go to live by herself in Rome. This decision made everybody mad at her. At that time, no one in Laura's town thought that a woman could live alone. The situation was unbearable. Her mother decided that it would be good for Laura and everybody else if she stayed with her brother Ross who lived in Canada with his wife and daughter. She wanted to leave her home, but she hated the idea of living in someone else's home even if it was her brother's house.

Laura made clear that she would stay in her brother's house for a while but that she would find an apartment and start a new life by herself.

Everything was done fast and legal, so in less than two months, Laura immigrated to Canada. She had a good job in Italy that she liked; but she had made up her mind and accompanied by her brother Demy on one sad morning, she went to the airport and left her home. She could never forget the day that she left her home for Toronto Canada. Her mother was in the kitchen weeping, her father had gone out because he could not bear to see her leave and Laura saw him leave the house weeping, he held his handkerchief while he shook his head. A half an hour prior to her departure everyone else found something important to do out of the house, as everyone left Laura became very nervous. She was so nervous that she wanted to go immediately, but she missed all of her family so much that she wanted to sit down and never leave. Demy took her by the hand and pulled her towards the door. She wept all the way to the airport.

At the airport, Demy gave her a present of a small green English/Italian dictionary that Laura still has and cherishes. She and Demy had a cup of coffee at the airport cafeteria and while drinking it, the airline invited all the passengers going directly to Montreal to board the plane. She got in line while Demy encouraged her, but Laura vividly remembers that she almost turned back and ran home three times but she did not. She had suffered the last three months living at home and she had become insufferable to her family. She was crying all the time. She became simply mean. She felt that everybody in her family wanted to get rid of her because she removed herself from the family's everyday life. Was it really so terrible being dumped by a man? Now she did not think so, but then she was devastated.

It all began when she was fourteen years old. It was a summer day in the country where the family spent the summer. Laura's older brother invited one of his friends to stay with us for a weekend. His name was Vance and he was very tall. He had black eyes, black wavy hair, and he joked a lot. He had a contagious laughter. His skin was darkish, maybe because of sun overexposure. He was constantly looking at Laura and she did not like it. Her first impression of him was not a favorable one. However, something strange happened to her. Every time she looked at him, she felt a tingling sensation, which was completely new to her. Laura thought that he was ugly, but she could not help looking all the time at him. He was a student of law and talked too much. Two days later, he left, but he took her young heart with him. In the weeks and months that followed, she thought of him and wished that he would come back to visit again, but he did not visit while the family was in that part of the country.

After we returned to the town, Laura saw him often enough and in a few short months she knew that she had fallen in love with him. At the age of fourteen, she was a full-blown woman. She had many suitors younger and older than her, which she could consider. One day she asked her older brother if it was all right if Vance courted her. Her brother became very angry and told her that he preferred Laura dead, rather than see her married to Vance. Vance had a very bad reputation; he was a womanizer and a liar. After that day, her parents forbade her to go out alone with him (it was the year 1950) and Vance never came to our house again. Laura was completely lost in love with Vance and could not understand what was wrong with him. Then she discovered what was wrong with him, He was agoraphobic.

It all started when the Italian government notified Vance that he must go thru a physical examination to serve in the army, but because he had not completed his academic study of law, he needed more time to graduate as a lawyer. In Italy, there is a law that stated that a student could postpone going to mandatory military training until he was twenty-six years of age in order to complete his studies. All fit Italians, after they reached their twenty-sixth birthday, had to participate in military training and service. Soon after his birthday, he received a letter scheduling his preliminary medical check-up that would determine whether he was fit for service. When he went for the medical check-up, he tried to convince the doctor that checked his physical condition that he was insane. The doctor looked him in the eyes and said, "Listen man you are trying to convince me that you are unfit to serve, so that you don't have to go into the army, but you don't have to try at all, because you are unfit to serve, truly unfit. You are insane!" The doctor dismissed him. When he came back home, he was bragging about how he fooled the doctor, and he celebrated his victory with all his friends. However, he started, in less than a month to think about what the doctor had said about his being handicapped by being unable to stay in open places and he eventually convinced himself that he was insane. Vance said to his parents, "If, as the doctor said, I am unfit, I am dangerous to anyone who forces me to go outside; I need to stay locked up inside. He is correct! I have always felt bad about being outside." After this realization, he found that he liked and felt safe in totally enclosed areas, so he refused to go out. The prayers of his mother and the orders of his irate father were all in vain. The doctors called his illness agoraphobia. He refused to go out and for fifteen years he stayed indoors. After all that time, a college hired him as a tutor because no one deemed an agoraphobic dangerous.

Laura never saw him again and her poor heart never healed from this impossible love. Vance loved Laura too, he spoke with her mother about being in love with her and he would make his intentions known to her after he became a lawyer. In those days, and especially for her family, the parents had to approve who dated a girl. Vance never kissed Laura, never touched her, but in their hearts, Laura and Vance acted betrothed. Then things changed for Laura because her family moved to the Northern most part of Italy (Lombardy). After the almost twenty years she was with Vance, Laura still refused to date anyone, but she was older, and her parents wanted her to marry. Laura finally realized that she was close to spinsterhood, so she started to date for the first time in her life.

However, an extraordinary thing happened. She had said no to so many suitors that she had lost count. Now, after she decided to say yes, things reversed themselves. As she said no to so many suitors before, now her suitors started dumping her. Everyone that she liked or dated found her to unemotional. She could not understand what was happening, she was only 35 years old and still beautiful or so many people told her. All the men that mattered to Laura or that she liked dumped her. Was it karma? Alternatively, was it because her parents taught her not to show love or passion to people she loved? The generation after the war in Italy showed their emotions more and did not like stoics that did not display the emotions that they felt. She just could not understand what had happened to her. What happened stunned her and made her very unhappy. It depressed her. She needed a change. She was sure of that.

Laura agreed to immigrate to Canada. Going to Canada would give her valid reason to leave her family. She planned to become fluent in English while staying in Ontario with her brother, and then she would go to Quebec and become fluent in French. She had studied both languages in college, but she could not think in either language. Therefore, she could not teach them at the university level. In the event that she failed and went back to Italy, she could teach the two languages at the university level. That was the contingency plan and all her family told her it was a good plan. It seemed like a very good idea and she was happy to do it, but it never happened.

Laura had never boarded a plane before, but she was not afraid. The plane, a jumbo jet, was so big and there were so many people on board. The seats were so close she was sure she would be uncomfortable. When she sat in her seat, she felt she was in a cage. Nevertheless, things very soon changed for the better. Her seat was the closest to the window. Two elder women occupied the other two seats on this side of the aisle. They were very talkative and laughed very often. When she first sat down, they annoyed Laura and she wished them away, but then they started to talk to her and, soon enough, she and her companions became friendly. As soon as the plane flew away from the airport, Laura experienced motion sickness for the first time in her life. She was so sick that she started to weep. Marta, the older of her two companions, came close to her and screamed with all the strength in her lungs next to her ear, "Laura, stop vomiting or I will kill you!" Marta spoke as if she meant it. Laura was speechless. She turned and looked at her. Marta looked at Laura with a joyous look in her eyes and a resplendent smile on her face. Believe it or not, after a small pause, Laura began to laugh, and she laughed heartily without understanding or knowing why. Laura just looked at Marta's face and could not stop laughing and then like a miracle Laura stopped vomiting and felt much better.

While Laura looked at her happy companions, Gina attempted to curtsy to her, although the seat belt restricted her in the seat. Gina said, "Mind over matter, your highness. Lady, you will never be sick again when traveling on an airplane." Laura never suffered from motion sickness again, even though she traveled back and forth to Italy many times. Laura's two companions were in their late sixties. Although they showed little signs of aging, they were still very pretty. They had black eyes and gray hair, they both wore eyeglasses, and a gold ring on each of their fingers to keep their eyes healthy and for good luck. The three of us talked a lot and Laura ended up telling them her story. "Laura you are very lucky to have been dumped by that scoundrel, men like your ex-boyfriend are better to lose than to find." A trip that Laura had envisioned mournful and tedious became the best she had ever taken. Laura never forgot Marta and Gina. After so many years, she remembered them with fondness and gratitude. She wished she had asked them for their address. Many times during the years after she met them, she often yearned to see and talk with them. At the Ottawa airport, her brother, his wife, Laura's little nice Rachel and Michael, the son of a Laura's cousin who was visiting Laura's brother, waited for her. They were very happy to see Laura and she was no longer sad and fearful. Her contingency plan to go back to Italy and teach English and French did not happen. After three years, Laura married. She married an American, and immigrated to the United State of America.

A Case of Revenge

iazza Filottete was at its busiest time of the day. It was a Saturday morning. People were going up and down the main road of Piazza (Plaza) Filottete. In their best attire of the week, the people talked and laughed while they went in and out of the many stores to do business. They carried parcels, just walked on the Marciappiedi (Walkway), or just had fun. People used one side of the road mostly as a meeting place. They met there to see friends, to discuss business, to exchange views on politics, to discuss the most important current events, and to talk about the life of the town in general. The survivors of the big earthquake built the town on a hilly promontory on the eighth of March about 579 BC, but no one knows which year it occurred for sure. Above the walkway, on a pedestal stood the statue of a hero or the founder of the town of whom I know very little about, by the last name of Filottete. Every week on the same hill, the area behind the statue became alive with the town market.

All of sudden the hubbub was stopped by a very loud screeching of tires that could be heard from the other side of Piazza Filottete. The driver of a large truck had lost control of it. He honked the horn while the truck came down the road. He was trying to avert an accident that could have been fatal. People were running towards the squealing tires from all around the piazza screaming, "Stop! Stop; don't hit the child!" A small girl child, terrified by what was happening, stood frozen in the middle of the intersection with her little hands up above her head. At that very moment, a courageous woman, who was close by the child, put her life in jeopardy. She tried to save the girl's life by picking her up and jumping back to the sidewalk just in time to avoid the truck.

The woman that saved my little three-year-old sister's life was still shaking and holding my little sister. She asked, "Who are the parents of this child?" Another woman in the crowd, after a small hesitation, answered, "She is the daughter of Mr. and Mrs. Pascos." The woman that still held my little sister dropped her unceremoniously on the ground, and screamed, "Oh no! God destroy them all! Had I known whose daughter she was, I would have let her die. I, as God is my witness, would not have picked her up." "Oh! Please, Constanza don't say that. She is just a child. She is innocent of any wrong doing," said another woman in the crowd. Still a very mad Constanza screamed, "You don't know what the Pascos did to me. They ruined my family and the honor of my daughter! All of them should pay for what they did to me. I will never forgive them."

By this time, the police had arrived to the site of the accident and four police officers were trying to disperse the crowd. Constanza was still upset but she had calmed down a bit and as soon as she spoke to the police officer, she left. The policeman, who was in charge, tried to thank her for her courage and good will, but Constanza ran away still cursing the Pascos family. My little sister crying with her hands still above her head called, "Mamma, mamma, help me." Unobtrusively, my sister was trying to disappear into the crowd to go home in a hurry and avoid punishment for going out alone in the street, but one of the policemen, who continued to arrive, recognized her. He picked her up and said, "I know you, young lady. I will take you home myself," exclaimed Martino. My little sister knew the policeman very well too. She exclaimed in tears, "Martino, I am so happy you are here. But please, please don't take me home. My mother will punish me if you do." "Good," answered Martino. "I will help her punish you and I will put you in jail for three days as you disobeyed your parents. Young girls like you cannot go out in the street alone." The cunning little brat jumped in Martino's arms hugged him tight around the neck and crying on his shoulder whispered, "Martino, not to jail, please, I will never do it again. I promise!" Martino said, "OK, Doretta," Doretta is my sister's name, "I will not put you in jail for this time only! Do you understand me?" Doretta said, "Yes, Martino! Yes, never again!"

My parents worked in our store from eight in the morning to whenever they finished the day's work. Our store was on the other side of the street from the police station. All the town's policemen knew all of our family. When at the store, Martino didn't say anything to my mother in front of Doretta. Doretta as soon as she felt safe put on an incredible show. To save herself from being punished, she began to cry and after sobbing violently, she said, "Mamma, oh mamma! Someone almost ran over me with a truck. My mother stopped what she was doing and ran to see how she was. Doretta continued before her mother recovered from the news of the accident, "You cannot imagine, mamma, what the woman that saved me said! She said, in front of everybody in the plaza, that if she knew that I was your daughter, she would have left me to die! Can you imagine that?" At this point, she started to cry with longer fake sobs. My mother could not believe what she had heard. She was too upset even to think of punishing Doretta. The thought that her little girl was in an accident and needed her help, forced her, at least for the time being, to forget Doretta's grave infraction. Then people came into the store to shop and Doretta happily went in the back of the store to play.

I was always amazed of how easily my little sister could get out of troubles. It was, may be, because she was the youngest, my parents were more forgiving towards her. That night our parents found it important to explain, not condone, to the older of their children the frightening adventure of our little sister.

Aunty Nett, one of my father's sisters, was a tall well-fed woman. She had an oversized neck due to a thyroid deficiency, but she had a pretty round face and big brown eyes. She was religious in her own way. Saint Anthony of Padua was her patron saint, and she prayed to him with fervor every day. For this reason, she expected her patron Saint would solve all her problems. Because she was devoted to her religion, we believed whatever she said. My aunty was self-important. She had the capacity to argue and defend her point of view like a trial lawyer, a very femininc girl lawyer. She was married to an expert homebuilder. She had five children - two boys and three girls that she adored. The first boy, whose name was Francis, was very handsome and he was as talented as his father was. The women liked him and he enjoyed courting them very much, maybe too much. Amongst the girls that he enjoyed courting, he seemed to prefer a beautiful young girl by the name of Amelia. Amelia was one of Constanza's daughters. Constanza was the woman that saved my little sister from the car accident at the plaza. While Francis enjoyed flirting with Amelia, Amelia fell seriously in love with Francis. Unfortunately, Francis did not realize that Amelia was serious about him and when he did realize that Amelia was serious, it was too late. In fact, Amelia made clear to Francis that she wanted to marry him.

Francis did not entertain any intention of marrying Amelia; she was just a flirt to him and tried to end the relationship. Amelia would not have it. She would write long letters to him, she would follow him, and she would

make scene when he refused to go with her. She was totally lost and in love with him. When Amelia found out
that Francis had a girl friend, and that Francis' parents
approved of her, she completely lost it. She told her parents that Francis had raped her. He may have raped her,
but no one could know for sure. In those days, rape was
an unforgivable crime for the whole family. The act was a
disgrace that only marriage could repair. Francis denied
having sex with her. He admitted courting her but swore
to God that nothing physical happened between the
two of them. Constanza believed her daughter. When
she realized there was nothing that would force Francis
to marry Amelia, she went to the police to report the
alleged rape to save her daughter's honor.

Because Amelia was still under eighteen years of age,
the police arrested Francis and put him in jail. Lawyers
were hired. A terrible legal battle began which annoyed
and distressed all the concerned parties. As we always
told everyone, our Store was very close to the police
station. Actually, it was just across the street from the
station. Because the police station was so close to our
store, there was a certain amount of amicability between
my parents and the police. Because people thought my
father to be a man of influence in the town, in their
ignorance and selfishness, they believed that he could
ask for anything or ruin anybody even if it was wrong
and unjust. Because the police released Francis from jail
after a week, Constanza thought that the relatively quick
release was due to my father's influence with the police.
She went around the town telling everyone who listened

to her that the police freed Francis because my father was a friend of the police. This accusation was false. She also accused my father of bribing the doctor that checked Amelia for sperm activity. Later Constanza accused my father of bribing the jury because of the trial's outcome. Only she believed the wild accusations.

The trial took place in the city of Catanzaro the capital of the region. My father did not have any friends there. The only thing that my father could have done to help was to have Francis released from jail earlier. My father denied it and I believed him. My father tried to talk Francis into marrying Amelia even though he believed that Frances did not rape the girl. He tried to save the honor of both families. Francis would not do that and the war between the families continued. Before and after the trial the town's populace divided equally about the matter. Some people thought that Amelia was so much in love with Francis that she fabricated the whole thing to marry him. Other people thought that Francis was an arrogant womanizer and although they believed Francis innocent, they thought that he well deserved his troubles for all his arrogance.

Constanza could not believe that verdict would be not guilty and she needed a scapegoat. She found it by accusing my father who fought with my aunt to have Francis to marry Amelia for the sake of the family honor. My aunty Netty was adamant, she believed that her son was innocent and he should not marry Amelia. While the trial was still going on my aunty came to our house screaming at us and cursing my father when he did not agree with her and refused to intervene to have her son released from jail before the due date. My father tried to settle the dispute amicably with both parties; instead, he became the enemy number one to both sides. My aunt harassed us for not agreeing with her and not freeing her son from jail until the trial ended. When Constanza disagreed with the trial's outcome, she firmly believed that the result was because my father bribed everyone who acquitted the man that brought dishonor to her daughter and her family. My father said, "It was not true!" Most of the people in the town knew some of the many that she accused of dishonorable acts. They knew that Constanza's anger at the trial's outcome and her love of her daughter spoke without regard for the people who were involved in the trial and the dispute.

I never understood either my aunt or Constanza. When there are no witnesses to an act, people cannot take the word of one party or the other. Both parties are big losers because no one can determine the truth. It lays somewhere between the two versions of the events. Unless there is a lie and someone uncovers the truth or the accused has irrefutable proof of his or her innocence, no one can say what happened. No one of the people involved can ever be sure of what exactly happened. Amelia never married and Constanza thought it was my father's fault. I think that both parties were wrong. Will the truth ever be known? We will never know.

A Killing of Jealousy

I *loved my small neighborhood. Our* neighborhood was about a quarter mile long and our street was fourteen feet wide. On each side of the street there was a row of flats. The flats were two stories high and very small. The street was paved with cobble stones. From the beginning to the end of the thoroughfare, the road was a very steep grade. Because of the steepness of the hill, every 5 feet or so there was a large step in the road to stop people from running and stop carts and buckboards from using the road without restrictions during the winter when there was ice on the street. The left side of our house stood between via Fiumicelli and via Pastorelli. The rear of the house abutted another house, the front of the house stood in piazza San Francesco. A vegetable garden and a brand new theatre was on the left side of the square where our house was, while another row of flats was on the right side of the square. Opposite our house was a three story stone building with large spacious flats. On the first floor, there were commercial shops, which included a sculpture studio and three small food and variety stores. The road in the square had a smooth concrete surface. The front of our house took up the full length of our side of the Piazza and continued down to the church of San Francis of Paola.

Our house was three stories tall. All of the first floor was used by a school. An outside stairway led to the entrance of our flat on the second floor. The entrance lead a long entrance hall that lead to the kitchen and the bathroom on one side, a temporary storage area stood at the other end of the hall. At the center of the entrance hall, an entrance to our three bedrooms, and stairs went to a very large attic that took up the third story above the three bedrooms. Along via fiumicelli on each side there were two rows of smaller houses made of one big room and one bathroom per flat, very few flats had a kitchen. In our neighborhood the chickens and other small animals roamed free all over the place. The houses were one attached to the other without any space in between each house; it was like one long building. Because the flats were too small for the children to stay inside, all of them when not at school were out playing and making a lot of noise with their screams and laughter. The children slept in their parents' bed until they were 3 years old. After the child reached that age, the child switched to sleep in another bed in the same bedroom, two at the top of the bed and one at the bottom. In any bedroom, the children would always behave because the penalty for fighting was very heavy and painful.

During the day, the children spent their time in the street sitting down on the steps or on small chairs, playing or studying. The only inconvenience was that the children had to stop playing when people came down our street, so the kids had to clear the street to let the people pass. This would increase the children's roaring laughter. When some of the boys thought that they were unseen, they played stupid jokes on the people who passed them. The stupid jokes included sticking sticks between their legs and then denying everything when they were accused of it. The passerby at times laughed, at other times they would get mad and complain to any available adult. The children of the neighborhood would then accuse one another, which would create pandemonium until one mother would intervene to settle things down.

No adult wanted the children left alone. Some mothers and big sisters would take turns watching over them. The mothers and the big sisters would sit on the stairway to watch them play while chatting amongst themselves. While nursing the babies and the youngest of the children, they talked and gossiped. Most of the time, they enjoyed it and had a grand time. The last three hours of the day for the children that went to school were devoted to homework and getting ready to welcome their fathers home from work.

After dusk, this lovely picture would disappear. An incredible scene would replace that picture. The fathers would come home from work and if anything displeased them they would insult and often beat up the wives mercilessly. The men thought of themselves as the heroes and the bread winners of the home as if a woman's keeping house and raising the children was not hard enough. I was indignant and my mother was always watching after me to avoid my running out to scream and tell those brutes my peace. I, simply, could not understand then, nor could I understand now, why the women would take the beating. They would just be screaming and sobbing painfully. No one would dare to go to help. Sometimes someone would call the police, but the women would deny everything.

I can still remember a lovely woman by the name of Catherine. She was 8 months pregnant. An Ambulance rushed her to the hospital one night because of the beating her husband had given her. She had seven children between the ages of eleven and twenty years old. Her children were completely subdued by their father and they stood silent unable to intervene when he beat their mother. After the last beating, a neighbor called the police, but she, as usual, told the police that her many bruises were the result of a bad fall. She, after a month died suddenly and no one did anything for her. Few months later, the brute got married again to a woman of another town. When he brought the new wife home I remember I cried. And to this day I remember her with fondness. To my estimation, these kinds of men are paltry, arrogant, ignorant, and cruel. Any kind of violence brings destruction, pain, shame, and a bad example.

In my neighborhood, another family that concerned

me was the sheepherders who were quieter than most. The family consisted of the parents, three boys and one girl. They were a family of shepherds. They kept by themselves and seldom spoke to anyone. I was very young, but I think I had a crush on all three boys. They were so handsome and dressed with decorum. Their names were Jerome, who was 20 years old, Luigi, who was 22 years old, and Carlo, who was 25 years old. The girl's name was Lucy; she was eighteen years old, the mother, Rosaria, and the father, Anthony, were in their mid fifties. The father was tall and had regular features except that he had a nose that was too long. The mother was blond and very beautiful, although she showed the marks of having lived a very hard life. All the boys worked out of the town and in the country. At night they would come back home and I, always, looked for them. I just wanted to look at them. Was I smitten with them? Maybe I was, but I don't think so. All three were of the same height; they had fair skin, blond curly hair and the most beautiful blue eyes. Rosaria, their mother had noticed my admiration for her sons and went to see my mother to tell her, to let me know that I was making a fool out of myself because I was just a child.

Soon after her visit, my mother called me into the bedroom where we could hope to have some temporary privacy because all my other siblings were out playing. My mother put me on her lap and told me that it was wrong for a young girl to go to look at men, especially young men, "But why momma," I answered. "I like them, they look like angels. I just like to look at them I don't ask anything." She answered, "I know you mean well but you see my girl, if a woman looks men in the eyes, even if they are young, they think that the woman wants to marry them." "Do you want to marry a shepherd?" "I don't want to marry anybody," I answered really mad. "I know better." My mother said, "You are too young to think about these matters." Before my mother left, she kissed me. Then she said, "don't worry my girl! You learned something new." I did worry for a while. I thought that I had escaped a great danger because I believed that husbands were bad people who beat their wives. I was scared that by looking at all three of them, I would have to marry all three of them. I said, "I don't want to be beaten by all the three of them! I will never look them in the eyes again." My God, I didn't know it.

As it happened, I did not see the three young men for a long time because a terrible tragedy happened, to the family, soon after my mother spoke to me about them. The thought I would have to marry them so scared me that I never looked them in the eyes anymore. For that matter, I never looked any men in the eyes for years. Every morning I remember waking up to the sound of sheep and goat bells, at which time my older brother would jump out of bed and run to get the milk for our family. A large number of sheep and goats led by the three shepherds and their mother would go around the town to sell their milk. The shepherds would squirt the milk, in front the customer, from the goats or sheep's teat, in large round containers then they would fill the bottles of their customers with a measuring cup. Which kind of milk our mother would want us to have I don't remember, sheep or goats milk, I mean. What I remember is the nice smell and the warmth of that fragrant milk. The reason why I looked them in the eyes, before the incident of having to marry one of them, was that I knew them. I bought their milk and brought it home for all in my family to drink. I thought that the shepherds, also, sold the most delicious tender ricotta cheese in the world.

We, my family and I, were living in the South of Italy. After moving from our little town into northern Italy, I never had the pleasure to eat fresh ricotta cheese like that again. The Shepherds were, besides looking like angels, the most strange and interesting people that I ever knew. The father was tall and had regular features but he had too long of a nose, the mother was blond and very beautiful, although she showed the marks of having lived a very hard life. The daughter looked like her father nose and all. All of them kept pretty much by themselves, with the exception of their closest relatives that they often met after work in her home. One of these relatives was a cousin named Michael. He was married to a beautiful girl named Juliana. Nevertheless, Juliana previously had a failed engagement with his brother Carlo. This was often the cause of quarrels and scenes of jealousy between Michael and Carlo. He liked to drink, and when drunk he would go to the shepherds house to remind Carlo to leave his wife alone. Even though nobody could prove that Carlo and Michael's wife had an affair, people continued to talk about the frequent encounters taking place between the two of them.

Michael was very much in love with his wife and very jealous. He was always sensitive about his wife associating with any man. On a very cold winter day after dark Michael thought or was told that his wife and Carlo had met. He was drunk at the time, and, without thinking clearly, he went to Carlo's house to defend his honor. Once Michael got to Carlo' house he started to tell Carlo to leave his wife alone and that he would not permit any more clandestine encounters. Carlo answered him that he hadn't seen his wife for a long time, and that Michael must go home and go to bed, but Michael would not listen to reason and started a quarrel. Michael accused Carlo of having an affair with his wife while Carlo denied any wrongdoing. Violence erupted with punches, verbal insults, and all sorts of accusations after a few minutes. Then Carlo drew his knife. At one point Carlo and several members of his family knifed Michael several times. Some people said that even the women took part in the killing. Carlo and the family threw Michael out of Carlo's house into the street bleeding and screaming. Michael got up and tried to go home but the pain was so excruciating that he could not help himself from weeping and loudly moaning.

It was dark. My poor mother having worked all day at the store was on the balcony of our house watering the flowers. Upon hearing and seeing the man suffering such pain my mother asked, "What is wrong young man? What happened? Can I help you?" He stopped lifted his head up and looking at my mother emitted a long heart breaking sob and fell down on the street. My mother ran inside the house calling my father! "Pat, Pat, hurry up and go out to the plaza. There is a badly hurt man. I think he just collapsed." My father ran out immediately. Nevertheless, by the time he reached where the man fell, many other people had come to help. Six men had gathered the poor man into a sheet, and they ran carrying him to the doctor. By the time they arrived at the doctor, Michael had died.

My mother could not water the flowers on the balcony for a long time. She would remember and seemingly see with sorrow the terrorized eyes and the pain of the man in the street. Could this tragedy have been avoided if Michael had not been drunk? We will never know. All the people of the town were outraged. Everybody thought that the shepherd's family should have shown mercy for poor Michael.

There was a week of mourning in the town. No one could believe that the shepherd's family could kill so brutally one of their own. Carlo and Jerome assumed responsibility for the killing. They went to jail for a few months. Pending the trial, the parents of the two killers got them the best lawyer they could find. After six Months, the police released them because Michael provoked the fight. It was clear that poor Michael had gone to Carlo's house to fight for Juliana because everybody thought that she was guilty of infidelity. Everyone shunned her and many times people threw stones through her window at her. She denied any wrongdoing, but she had to leave town in the end. In those days, society punished with death any woman for infidelity.

My Life with Dogs

I am not a lover of dogs but in the course of 25 years I have had three dogs. It all began in the summer of 1980, on a bright Sunday morning. The door bell rang and I opened the door to find, David, the young son of my friend Pat who stood in front of me with a worried face and imploring eyes. He was holding a new born black puppy with a white streak in the middle of his head. The puppy was shaking and whining, but David was trying to remember a prepared speech to tell me. "Teresa", he started, "I need a big favor from you, please! help me, "sure David tell me what I can do for you and I will help you" "You see Teresa I found this puppy in a trash can, he was crying and scratching the trash can while he tried to get out of it. I could not possibly leave it there to die, please take it and care for it, please! My mother won't let me keep it." David started crying.

I invited him into the house because I could see that the puppy was dying of starvation. I gave the puppy some milk that the puppy promptly drank, and then I started telling David that I was very sorry but I did not care for dogs very much. I told him that I did not like to have small animals in my kitchen. Nevertheless, David did not take no for an answer, he continued to cry. He told me that I would not have to keep the puppy in the house since I had a big backyard. "I will build a dog house for you; you will only have to give him food and water! Please, Teresa I beg you don't let him die."

To tell you the truth, I was troubled and annoyed. The little puppy was still so hungry that he was sucking on David's shirt. David was an 8-year-old boy. He was very handsome, he had big blue eyes and longish blond hair, I liked him very much, and his stress and love for the puppy conquered my heart. I could no longer say no and to David's delight I caved in and said "yes!" He was so happy that he dropped the puppy on the floor and hugged and kissed me. David kept his promise and within 24 hours, with his father's help, he built a nice new little doghouse.

I now had my first dog. We, my husband and I, named it Rex. I believed that because Rex did not get the training and love he deserved, Rex grew up to be disobedient and always on the run. By that time, I found that I loved Rex; my husband also loved him. Eventually Rex became too much for us to handle. Mary and Art, two good friends of ours decided to move to Biggs where they had bought a kiwi farm. They knew how stressed we were about having to care for Rex, they asked us if we would give Rex to them, to be with them on the farm.

Because we loved Rex, after some debating about Rex's life on a farm, we decided that because Rex would play with lots of children in a larger space, Rex would have a better life on Mary and Art's farm. We, my husband and I, accepted. Naturally, before Rex left, we informed David of our decision. He said to us that as long as Rex was taken care of it was OK with him. As it is always the case, when somebody is no longer around we tend to forget the bad things and remember only the good ones, I was surprised that I ended up missing Rex very much.

A week later, on a Sunday, my doorbell rang. When I opened the door, I did not expect what I saw. I could not believe it! David held another young dog in his arms again at our door. "Oh no! NOT AGAIN"! I cried. Nevertheless, David with his big imploring eyes said, "Please Teresa", he told me with emphasis, "This is a good one!" "He will not give you any problems." "He is almost trained and he is not a whiner. The Vet neutered Rex for us. So, he will not travel about the neighborhood. Please give this dog three days, and if you still do not want him I will pick him up. You already have a big dog house and he will be no trouble at all." The love of this boy for any kind of animal touched me. Pat, his mother, had previously told me that her backyard was full of strays of all kinds David had even brought skunks home. We named this dog Rex too. Rex was playful, affectionate, and a good watch dog. We soon became fond of him, but because we did not let stay him inside the house, Rex would get upset and bark at us. Rex started to run around the neighborhood and stayed out for hours. Rex would return for food or sleep. He always came home every night. He always sneaked into his dog house surreptitiously pretending that he never had gone out. One day while I was cooking in the kitchen, I heard a loud noise on the street in front of the house. The driver of a car after hitting Rex was trying to run over his body again to escape. I ran out screaming: "Stop! Stop!" "You are killing my dog." He stopped for a moment to steer the front wheels to the right and drove away. Rex expired in my arms moments later. I was grief stricken. I could not believe that anyone could do such a thing. Even to a dog. Desperately hoping that he could be revived, I rushed Rex to the veterinary clinic. He was dead! The only thing I could do was to make arrangements for Rex to be cremated and his ashes returned to us. Rex is buried in our backyard under a rose bush. He was 6 years old.

I was missing Rex a lot, and then a coworker came into my office with a big smile. She told me, "Teresa, a friend of mine had a litter of 4 puppies. Would you like to adopt another puppy?" "Yes," I said, "I really would like to have another dog." Next weekend we drove to Oakley to pick up the puppy. They all were so handsome. My friend insisted that she choose the puppy for me. She said, "Teresa, This dog is the cutest of the bunch. You are going to love him!" She did not take the dog herself because her young son had chosen a girl puppy, her son wanted to have more puppies of his own. We named the puppy Ulisse after my mother's dog in Italy. Ulisse's fur coat was a medley of white, clear red, and brown. His head was half white and half reddish brown, his muzzle was predominantly reddish brown touched with white spots, his legs were all white, while his upper body half reddish brown and half white. He was a mix between an Australian red healer and a beagle. Ulisse on our way home peed and vomited on me several times. I discovered we shared another trait – motion sickness. Evidently the motion of the car did not agree with him. Having forgotten that I could not have pets inside the house, I was faced with the same problem as with the other dogs. It was winter so Ulisse was too young to be left out at night. So we made a place for him in the laundry room, when the weather became warmer he moved to a better and bigger dog house. After a while he adjusted to it. Like my previous 2 dogs, Ulisse liked to run out on the street any time he could. He grew up to be a big dog. When, on weekends I took him for a walk, he would pull me forward to the point that I was required to run. It looked like that it was taking me out for a run and not vice versa. We should have taken Ulisse to obedience school but we did not do it and that was a big mistake. The dog grew up to be disobedient and a runner just like the prior two dogs. We faithfully took him to the vet who gave him all the prescribed medications. I would take him out for walks on the weekends and holydays because I worked full time. My husband was allergic to dog fur and could not help me care of him in the house. As Rex grew old, he did not run as much. Ulisse hated water and the dog was difficult to bathe. As soon as anybody brought a bath tray filled with water he would disappear. Every time I managed to bathe Ulisse, he would rub his skin on the ground (making a mess of his coat again) as soon as his bath completed. I loved Ulisse very much and I tried to compensate for keeping him outside the house by feeding the dog too much. For years I fed him one egg every day. Ulisse loved it especially the yolk.

All went well for 15 years, but then Ulisse got sick with a bad cough. The dog was showing signs of stress, so we took him to the vet. Ulisse was at the vet clinic for 3 days. After the dog came back home he was well for a while, but he got sick again with the same symptoms. I took him back to the vet's clinic. The vet kept him in the clinic for several more days and came up with a bad diagnosis, Bone Cancer! The dog must have an operation. The Vet did the operation but could not get all the cancer out.

Another year passed, Ulisse seemed OK and enjoyed the summer, fall, and winter. However, in the spring he started to limp and favor his left leg. We journeyed with him to the vet again, but this time the vet informed us that the cancer had metastasized into his leg bone. We were given a choice between putting him to sleep or keeping him alive and in pain for a couple more months. My husband and I were devastated; we chose to take him home for as long as he was not in pain. Ulisse was not the same dog anymore. His legs filled with sores. He could no longer run. We decided to take him back to clinic again to see if the vet could give him something to help.

When Ulisse and my husband left to go to the vet, I had bad premonition and started crying. My heart was telling me that I would not see Ulisse alive again. Before Ulisse left with my husband, I kissed him. A long interval passed without news, so I called the vet. The receptionist told me that the Vet was sure that Ulisse was in great pain. The Vet decided that because he was suffering too much, the best thing for Ulisse was to put him to sleep. Lee, my husband called me to tell that we had to let Ulisse go. I could not accept it and I told him to take it back home "Terry I cannot do it. I, also, love Ulisse. I promise you that I will stay with him through the last moment." I wanted to go and be there too, but my husband advised me against it. In the end, I stayed home crying my eyes out. Lee, when everything was ready, held Ulysses' front paws with one hand, while caressing his head with the other. Then the vet put Ulisse to sleep. When Lee came home, we cried over the passing of our at times naughty but splendid dog. Ulisse was 15 years old. He too is buried in our back yard under a fern bush. It has been few years, now, since Ulisse's passing, but I still miss him very much. We are not going to get another dog for two reasons. The first reason is that I am getting old and I would not be able to care for it. The second reason is that I could not go through the stress, emotional upset, and pain that I experienced when Ulisse died.

Summer Harvest

arvest is the most beautiful time of the year. The country at large acquires a golden rich color that speaks of bringing about the results and completeness of a job well done. The joy of having accomplished a beneficial deed for oneself and others. "Harvest", speaking this word transports me into a world of light and joy. Emotions enveloped me and filled me with joy and hope. As I speak this word, even on a cloudy day, I see sunshine with beautiful blue skies that are touched here and there by white, sparse, running clouds. I also see flowers, myriads of lovely colorful flowers on the streets, on the balconies, and on the farmers' windowsills. I see flowers that line the sides of the street, and some flowers in front lawns. Almost everywhere that there was a patch of unused ground, there were flowers. All these emotional visions created an aura of harmony and love. Whenever I feel this emotional vision, a lovely memory comes to my mind – the feast of St. Peter, which starts the summer harvest season.

On June 29 in our little town we celebrated the feast of the apostle San Peter. San Peter is the protector of friendship. On this day all girls either pledge or renew their friendship by becoming cummarris. A cummari is a person that forever, in the name of St. Peter, will love, help, and care for you. Every year the ritual is repeated. Large groups of young schoolgirls go around the town picking wild colorful flowers to make the bouquet (Mazzetti) of St. Peter that they will exchange with one another. After picking up the flowers, the girls would go home where their mothers or older siblings would help them prepare the bouquets (Mazzetti).

The bouquets were put on a tray draped with the most elegant piece of cloth that was available. A variety of candies and chocolates accompanied the bouquet. The girls would then go to other people's houses, where they would offer the bouquet and the sweets. They would renew the promise of their care, guidance, encouragement, aid, and friendship forever. The mother of the cummari would take the offering and, in return, fill the cummarri's tray with the ciambella of St. Peter. The ciambella was a pastry made with eggs, flour, sugar, vanilla, and olive oil. The ciambella was round and tall. On top of it there was a flower made of rich, sugared, white cream. It was very sweet. Right now, I can see it, and I wish I had the delicious yellow ciambella of St. Peter to eat. This is one of my loveliest memories of when I was so young and so happy.

As I looked out of the window, at the far away horizon, I remember how the summer harvest season graced the panorama all around. Far down the street, I could hear hired hands singing songs and laughing while they boarded the large coaches of the farmers who would bring them to their fields. Occasionally we heard the barking of a dog while the mule driven coaches transported everyone to the fields. The whole thing was so lovely that I wished I could always take part in it. Some years I missed the celebration, so in those years I imagined that I traveled with them on the coach while they laughed and sang. With my eyes closed, I could see large fields covered with yellow tall wheat, crowned on the top with long tresses of ripe grains, so vital to the support and well-being of our life. The wheat waved gracefully. It undulated under the caress of the morning breeze. A few times, I convinced my father to take me to a harvest site owned by farmers who were our friends. Once there I would work with them doing little chores. I was very happy then because for a few hours I would be part of the farmers' life while their children and hired hands would sing with the birds while scything the long blond stems of the wheat. All of us worked hard while they were making mounds of wheat. This would go on until after dusk. I remember standing by to listen until they would thank me and tell me to go home because my father had come to pick me up. Harvest will be a magic word and time for me because my family had something to harvest too. We had a vineyard in the country. We would harvest grapes to make wine between the end of

September and the beginning of October. Our vineyard was not very big, but my father produced enough wine for the needs of our extended family. My father produced two kinds of wine. Red wine made with blackish grape, and white wine with white grapes. It took a lot of preparation. My parents would close the store, which we had in town for a week. We spent the first three days cleaning the many containers needed to hold the "most" that was the juice that came out of the grapes. Our harvesting of the grapes was a family affair. We did not hire harvesters. The harvesters were people that were specialized in the picking up bunches of grapes and then smashing the grapes with their feet by jumping up and down on the grapes. Harvest day was the most joyous time for both my family and mc. Friends and family would be invited by my parents to enjoy the harvest time with us we all gathered on the day of the harvest until we numbered about 20 in all. My mother would stay in the summer house to prepare food for all of us and to take care of the youngest children of her large family. She also had the job to prepare her older children to do our share of work to make the "most" of the grapes. This was not an easy task, because she had to dress the six of us for the job and, after we stopped working, she had to clean our clothes and us. She had to prepare for our fighting after we finished crushing the grapes by preparing large buckets of water to be ready to cool us off and wash off the grape juice after the fighting happened. The fights happened every year, but not all of the family who crushed the grapes took part in the fighting. I remembered that there were six of us ready to work. She would dress the six of us with just a pair of shorts and then march us to the crushing shed while the others would pluck the grapes from the plants. After plucking, the grapes were in large wicker containers and we brought the filled containers into the crushing shed, where we put the grapes into a large cement basin to crush. As we crushed the grapes, the juice would drain into another cement container built under the first. The crushing shed or parmiento was the size of a small room, and so were the containers in the shed. Once there our mother would have us wash our feet and then we would go into the first container to jump on the grapes and swish out the juice that would drain into the other container. My father would stay around to watch us and to intervene when a fight happened. He was always ready for the many times when a fight broke out between the grape crushers. Usually every year, it happened. For a few hours, we would jump high and low on the grapes. We crushed the grapes under our feet while singing and having a lot of fun. Nevertheless, as it usually happened, one of us would drop a pail of dripping grapes on the head of the smallest child who would fall into the squashed grapes while screaming and crying to our mother for help. We never knew who dropped the grapes, but the rest of us would accuse one another. My father was ready to intervene but he waited to see if anyone would admit who started the fight. "It was you!" one would say, but another would say, "No way, it was you!" while pointing, pushing, and kicking. This would continue while everyone accused another until we were a tangle of arms and feet. All trying to catch the guilty one. No one succeeded because grape juice is slippery and everyone ended up pushing someone else. Since we could not reach a consensus about who did it and no one would admit to starting it, our father ended it by trying to pull his six angels (all colored dark red and dripping with grape juice) out of the crushing shed. He would rush towards us screaming. "Stop! Stop it you little scoundrels!" He would try to get one or two of us at one time, but all of us were retreating towards the end of the grape-crushing shed. All of us still screamed, "It was you! It was you!" In the end my father would catch us one or two at the time and put us in the waiting buckets of water. My mother being on the alert would rush immediately to help my father. My mother would care for all the children and then while looking at father say, "it is the same every year isn't it?" My father would smile and answer, "I wouldn't miss it for anything in the world." After a hard day of labor, all of us (both family and our friends) would sit at a big table to eat, drink, and talk about the day's adventures. After eating, we would lay on the grass and under the stars. All the adults would exchange news, tell jokes and recount stories. This night was the first night of the harvest, my uncle Antonio told us the story of the oil jar.

"The story goes this way," my uncle would say. "There lived in the town of Petronase a gentleman known for his avarice and hostility. He was a producer of olive oil. He had huge terracotta containers where he stored the oil after the harvest of his olives. That year because his harvest of olives promised to be very big he bought a very large container, the largest that anyone had ever seen. On the first day of the harvest of the olives he found his container broken in the middle. He stood speechless for a while, and then he started screaming, cussing, and cursing everybody. He threatened to go to the police and have all of them arrested. One of his workers staying at distance from him screamed to him that he knew someone who was very good at fixing all kinds of terracotta containers. Don Lollo, that was his name, stood silent for a moment then said to the man "go get him." The man hurried out and within an half of an hour he was back with a skinny old man who wore glasses and carried a small box with his tools. Don Lollo ran to the man asking him if he was good enough to fix his container. The old man answered that he knew what he was doing and if he did not like him he would leave. Don Lollo didn't answer and proceeded to show the little man, whose name was Toby, the container. Toby entered the container when Don Lollo asked Toby what he would do to fix it. Toby said, "I will glue all the pieces together". Toby started putting the pieces together assembling the container in a very precise and careful manner. In less than an hour he had joined all the pieces together with some glue. All this happened while Toby was still in the container. Toby showed Don Lollo how perfect the container was; he knocked all over it, the container sounded like new. Don Lollo was very happy and complimented him. Toby asked to be paid and Don Lollo was so happy that he gave him a bonus. Then Toby tried to get out of the container. He found out that he had assembled himself into the container with no way to escape. He screamed at Don Lollo to let him out. However, Toby told him that he fixed the container so well that only way out was to break the pot again. All Don Lollo's employees started laughing, and joined hands in a circle. They began to dance around the container still laughing, while Don Lollo continued to scream and cuss everybody. Then Don Lollo, green with bile, tried to catch one of the dancers. Both Don Lollo and his catch fell on the pot and broke the container while his employees continued to laugh at him. My uncle's story ended with loud laughter from all of us. But after few comments on the beautiful starry night we went to bed to rest and be ready and on time to continue our harvesting tomorrow morning.

The Donkey's Ears

*T*he classroom was large and full of whispering students getting ready for the day's lesson. The four walls of the classroom were enriched with pictures; centered on the back wall of the room was a picture of the Pope. It was the most prominent, but to the right side of the Pope's picture was a picture of the king of Italy "Vittorio Emanuele the third, while on the left side there was the picture of the president of the country - Benito Mussolini. On the right wall there was a large map of the world, on the left wall there was a balcony. On the balcony there were many flower pots of multicolored geraniums. Beside the balcony at the other end to the wall was the entrance door. On the fourth wall which faced the student benches there was the teacher's desk, above the desk, on the wall there was a large Crucifix of Jesus Christ. This day the classroom atmosphere was different because the homework would be corrected first thing in the morning instead of the afternoon like any other day. Mrs. Marie Delladonna the teacher, just as she would do any other day, had not taken from her big carryon bag her knitting work to knit for an hour or so while we were assigned to read in preparation of the day's lesson.

Mrs. Delladonna was a short fat woman; she wore her hair in a large bun behind her head, on the nape of the neck. The color of her hair was an ash blond, her large round face showed here and there small purple veins, and she wore large dark glass so the color of her eyes could not be seen. She always dressed in black and wore low heel shoes, she was a very mean teacher, who enjoyed punishing her students, and in short, she was a sadist and a very dishonest person. Above all, she enjoyed humiliating the students, especially the girls, that afterwards she would blackmail into going to her home to do house cleaning like washing the dishes, cleaning her dirty clothes, washing the floors and dusting, without compensation because, as she told them, she would be lenient when correcting their homework or questioning them. On her large desk there was a large manila folder, a large flat wooden stick, a little sack of beans, and in a separate bag the ears of a donkey. (Donkeys were universally thought to be stupid). The donkey's ears were to be used on students that didn't do their homework. With a devilish smile, Mrs. Delladonna would put the donkey's ears on the head of the unfortunate student that was at fault. The two of her preferred students would take the student to other classes to be humiliated.

If a student was caught misbehaving, or he or she

was not paying attention they would be whacked with the large stick on the palm of their hands with brutal force, when writing a composition they would get a whack for each error they made. There were children that cried, others went into contortions and for the rest of the day they would put their hands under their armpits or on their bosom because their hands hurt so much they could not use them. The children were ashamed to tell their parents, because the parents would side with the teacher because invariably the parents would receive a bad report regarding the child behavior and study progress. At other times, Mrs. Delladonna would put the students on their knees with hard dried beans under them for hours. It is important to note that; none of this torture was inflicted to the student of well to do parents because they were better educated, when they too misbehaved Mrs. Delladonna pretended not to see anything.

Occasionally an inspector would come to see how things were, but she knew it well in advance to make sure that everything would be all right. After the inspector left there were a lot of cries, and at this time the students, mostly the boys, were being punished for whispering to one another while the inspector was in the classroom. Only once did she NOT hand out punishments after an inspection. This happened because the inspector made her weep. We didn't know why she wept as they spoke with a very low voice. Most of the students thought that some of the parents had complained with the director about her cruel and most of the time unjustifiable punishments. We could not show it but we were happy that finally she got what was long overdue to her.

Risa was a shy well behaved student, she smiled a lot and the boys like to tease her because her clothes were not always clean and in order, she had big eyebrows and long black hair, she was small and thin and very good looking, her parents were shopkeepers and both worked long hours at their shop. The shop was a very large room divided in nooks. In the first nook they sold golden jewelry, in the second nook they sold guns and ammunition, in the third nook, which was, believe it or not, the largest of the three compartments; there was a food market. Mr. and Mrs. Pat Sopisco, Risa's parents were very busy from eight in the morning to nine o'clock at night. Pat Sopisco was a tall thin man with blue eyes and a large crop of white hair, he was a very active man who it seemed was never tired.

Mrs. Chiara Sopisco was of medium height, she was quite plump, and totally devoted to her family and her store, she had blond hair that she kept in a bun pinned to the nape of her neck and green eyes. She dressed simply but neatly. When she was young she was seen as a true beauty. At the time Mr. & Mrs. Sopisco had seven children, five boys and two girls, aged from thirteen years to one year old and to care for them and the store was really hard. Two younger sisters of Mrs. Sopisco that were not married helped her out most of the time but, still, she was not good enough to take care of all of them. One of her two sisters, Cloye, was very beautiful; she was of medium height with brown eyes and ebony black air. Teresa, the second sister, was not so beautiful, but she was gentle, kind, and worked very hard. She was short and thin, she had pale blue eyes and blondish air like Mrs. Sopisco. Teresa when still a child was very beautiful but when she was 5 years old she had a fall that scared her out of her wits. She never recovered from the injuries to her face. The injuries never healed completely. The injuries emotionally scarred her, so her beautiful little face changed so that people no longer saw her as beautiful. The children loved her and she was totally devoted to them.

When the two aunts could not come to help, all hell would break loose in the house. The boys would fight and all of them ended up going to school unprepared and late, the women that Mrs. Sopisco would hire to help were unable to deal with the children who they would say, were unruly and disobedient and would swear to never come back and some of them never did. On one of the days that the aunts could not come to help care for the children Risa had to help out working in the house all day, practically caring for everybody, she had to cook too. Once Risa at the end of a day keeping house and caring for the children was so tired that she forgot to do her next day's homework. In the morning Risa, knowing what the punishment would be if she went to school without doing her homework, tried to convince her aunts that she was sick and could not go to school that day. Aunt Cloye checked her temperature, and because she didn't have a fever and seemed to be ok. She was sent to school. To Risa their refusal to let her stay home meant she would be punished for caring for her brothers and sisters. In Risa's family school and education were very important because her parents wanted that their children be professionals when they grew up. In her family, excuses not to go to school were not accepted but were severely punished especially by her father.

For a child like Risa hiding was unthinkable, besides where would she go? Anybody that would see her in the street would call her father. The thought occurred to her that since the teacher's family were customers of her parents, and she never punished the children of the rich, maybe, even if her parents were not very rich, she would make an exception for her. Also, usually the boys were punished. Risa wanted to avoid the horrible punishment that waited for her. My God, she thought, I will be the first girl in her class to get this humiliating punishment. Risa didn't have any choice and weeping went to school. After the hour in preparation of the day's lesson had passed the teacher asked the students to bring their homework to her desk to be corrected.

Risa did not go. She stayed trembling in her seat at her bench and didn't dare look at the teacher. After a moment, the teacher got up from her chair. With the usually devilish smile on her face she said, "Class, I think that we will have a show today. Ms. Risa Sopisco did not do her homework today," then she walked to Risa's bench took her by one ear, and lifted her up and pulled her nearby her desk. She then proceeded to open the bag with the donkey's ears. Risa knew she was lost.

In desperation, she started screaming, weeping, wetting her face with tears, and with terror said, "Please, Mrs. Delladonna, please listen to me. I could not do my homework because I had to take care of my brothers and sisters. My aunt did not come to care for us. I had to take care of all of the family; I had to do everything from cooking and cleaning to overseeing my brothers and caring for the babies. Please do not do this to me! Forgive me. It will never happen again. It was not my fault. I do not want to wear the donkey's ears. I like to do my homework. Please, please forgive me," continued Risa.

By now, Risa had become hysterical and went on screaming louder and louder; she kept saying "please forgive me, forgive me." The students were all speechless and a terrible silence had descended on the classroom. Only the terrified screams of the shaking Risa broke the silence. Then the next door teacher came in to see what was happening. At that moment, the smiling Mrs. Delladonna tried to put the donkey's ears on the head of the screaming and pleading Risa. Then another teacher entered in the classroom. Mrs. Delladonna froze and let go of Risa who ran to her seat continuing to sob. The children who had been teasing and laughing at Risa were now silent like in a trance. Only the class heard the heart breaking sobs of Risa.

Risa did not get the donkey's ears but stayed at home with high fever for three days. Because Risa was terribly ashamed of what had happened did not tell her parents anything. For months the other children kept on teasing her, laughing at her and pointing at her in the street if they happened to encounter her, mimicking the episode of the donkeys' ears. How utterly cruel, sometime, children can be. Mrs. Delladonna the same day that Risa came back to school sent her to her home to do the house cleaning.

Risa was too embarrassed to tell her parents of the inhuman punishment that the teacher tried to inflict upon her, but she did tell them about having to do the teacher housecleaning three times a week. Both parents were outraged, her father especially was furious and wanted to report the teacher to the school director, but her mother voted against it because she thought that in the end Risa would fare badly considering how dishonest Mrs. Delladonna was. Nevertheless, they forbade Risa to go to the teacher's house to do her housecleaning anymore. Risa kept on going as she was terrified at the thought that the episode of the donkey's ears could repeat itself again. Risa, at the end of the academic year, passed to the next class even though she did not learn much. She was not happy but she knew that the next year she would request to be assigned to another class with a better teacher or so she hoped. Things changed for Risa but not in the way she thought it would.

Soon after the closing of the school year, her mother gave birth to her eighth child, a baby boy. One of her aunts got married, and the other aunt that came to her house to help her mother raise the children had to stay home to care for her invalid mother, she could come to help only twice a week. So, Risa had to take care of the baby and the house for three days a week. During the summer Risa took complete care of the baby doing what a mother or an adult person should do. On the other hand with such big family both parents had to work. Hiring a nanny was not economical possible, and besides no one would take care of a family of ten members eight of which were children. Risa grew attached to her little brother and enjoyed taking care of him. But when her parents called her and very apologetically told her that she could no longer go back to school because they needed her to continue to take care of the baby and the house for the time being, she was devastated. She cried, pleaded, and begged her parents to let her go to school with no good results. Her parents would say, "You know Risa that we have to work every day, your aunts cannot help us as much anymore, so, you must help us. The talk would always end with this statement, "for the time being you cannot go to school. Besides, we know what has happened to you at school and that you, against our will, went on playing maid to your dishonest teacher, so you might as well help us raise your brother and help all of us when your aunt cannot come to help." The reminder of Mrs. Delladonna and her horrible experience at school cooled her down a little. After thinking about it for a while, she said to herself, "A year or two will go by fast, I will study at home when I can. When I go back to school again, I will do two years in one and I will catch up very fast. Besides, I don't have to apply to change class to avoid going back to the classroom of Mrs., Delladonna." Still it was very hard for her because she wanted to become a doctor. She didn't want to waste time, but there was nothing she could do but accept her fate and do the best she could for her family.

Risa's parents had two more children; fortunately her aunts took three of the youngest children to their home but not Sal the baby she was taking care of. Risa had to wait until she was an adult to go to a recovery class program. She did not become a doctor; she became a teacher herself. Risa never forgot the donkey's ears episode. It left in her heart a deep painful scar. For many years, she had nightmares; she would wake up screaming, "forgive me Mrs. Delladonna forgive me." Her mother would rush to her bed to comfort her and calm her down, but she would go on weeping for the rest of the night. After few of those horrific nightmares Risa had to tell her parents what had happened at school regarding Mrs. Delladonna wanting to put on her head the donkey's ears because she hadn't done her homework. Her parents at first were mad at her for not telling them at the time it had happened. Then her mother wept while kissing and comforting her. Her father rushed out to go to the director's office to report the dishonest and cruel conduct of Mrs. Delladonna. The director apologized and promised her father that he would make sure that the teacher would be reprimanded and that something like that would never happen again to any child. We never knew what he did but my parents noticed that no one of Mrs. Delladonna's family came to the shop again.

Now that so many years have gone by Risa cannot

understand or forget what was happening in the school system to allow something like that to happen. Were they all insane? It is well known that in the early years of the 20th century most of the children especially if they were poor were treated as chattels but, Risa still asks herself, how could something like that happen? Was just that one teacher insane? How cruel can a person be towards another person? Certainly torturing a child is beyond the pale. Risa was only an eight-year-old child. Even now that Risa is a retired person, she still has nightmares in which she sees herself on the brink of desperation, twisting her hands and weeping asking for forgiveness and reprieve for a crime that was cruelly inflicted on her.

Carol

A strange case of accidental death

*W*hen *Carol was born in* the city of Scarborough it had not snowed for 5 years. As the baby girl started crying and a proud father joyously announced, "It is a baby girl! It is a baby girl!" Meanwhile, a multitude of happy voices from inside and outside the house screamed, "It is snowing! It is snowing!" Large white flakes were coming from the sky dancing and twirling under a very soft breeze. All the outside mirth was because of the surprise snowfall. People were afraid to walk on the snow because they didn't want to corrupt the white brilliance of the snow that was already forming an immaculate blanket on the ground. Then bells of all the city churches started playing a joyous tune and everybody in the streets was singing, dancing, hugging, and kissing each other. In the house, where the little girl had been born, the happiness of the parents and the other members of the family matched the happiness of the people in the city's streets. The little girl was beautiful. She had stopped crying, and now her big blue eyes seemed to be looking at all of the family. After a while, she fell asleep. The parents named her Carol. Carol, by the standards of the town, was now part of a rich family.

The father, Mr. Frederick Stanton, was tall, thin, and good-looking. He liked to dress well and was a bit of a flirt. He was a rich landowner. He had a lot of property in and outside Norwick where they lived; he also invested in the stock market. He loved his wife and all the children, but Carol was special to him. From the first day of her life he felt that there was a special bond between him and his beautiful little daughter. He could not stay away from home for long without missing her. Mrs. Stanton was of noble descent, she was a very good-looking woman. She had married young, and she, by the age of twenty-one, had two children - a boy named Richard and a girl named Carol. She loved her husband very much and adored the children. Her family was her life. She never would tire of caring for them. They lived in a mansion with all possessions and amenities that money could buy. Mr. and Mrs. Stanton believed that the children should learn both how to be independent and how to support themselves when they became adults. No matter what their station in life, fate can find ways to change it. So the children went to school and as teenagers volunteered to work helping others in wide ranging activities.

Carol grew up to be a very beautiful girl. She liked

children and she would work mainly in preschools on a part-time basis, while Richard helped his father. Carol at the age of seventeen was a true beauty and had many admirers, but she didn't consider marriage very important although she liked to flirt a little. She liked to play sports, especially tennis at which she excelled, so much so that she won two local tournaments.

Carol was a free spirit; she liked her life as it was. She didn't believe in conventions and she wasn't afraid to do what she believed was right. The school years were the happiest years of her life. Carol studied with passion. Carol liked to study to enrich her mind. She wanted to be the best teacher in the world, she dreamed of creating and inventing a better and happier life for everyone. She wanted the world to be a better place because of her contributions. Carol liked music, especially classical music. She, also, loved to dance and she would never say no to an invitation to a party were she knew she could dance. From her mother's side she was an aristocrat. One of her aunts had a grandiose anniversary party where the highest nobility of the country were invited. The most exquisite chandeliers, tapestries, and furniture that all the guests admired adorned the ballroom. The orchestra, which was one of the best in the country, played beautiful and famous dance music that almost forced the people young and old to dance. The ladies, dressed in elegant fashionable dresses, wore the most precious jewelry. At times the brilliant lights and the shining jewels intermixed, creating a feast of shouting brilliant stars. All the ladies were so beautifully dressed and styled that they seemed beautiful even if they were not usually considered so. However, Carol was so elegant and so beautiful that everyone noted and admired her.

The men in their tuxedos and white shirts seemed to enjoy themselves exchanging dance partners as often as they could. Amongst the men there was a celebrated bachelor who was still young. Although he was not handsome, he was thin, tall and had a kind of jovial charm. His name was Jerome Kingsley. He was the Duke of Essex. It was known that he had a lover, but since his lover was married, the unmarried ladies did not worry. His grace Kingsley having an eye for beautiful ladies noticed Carol immediately, and he asked Carol's aunt who she was. When Carol's aunt told him that she was her niece, he immediately invited her to dance. He didn't fall in love with her but she had made a first good impression on him and he also liked her. She was young, vibrant, and beautiful. Of late, his grace Kingsley was thinking to find a bride as he was getting on in years. His family thought that it was high time for him to have children especially an heir for his great wealth. Carol remained unimpressed by his grace, she was nice to him but just because he invited her to dance, in fact, after the dance, Carol did not think of him at all.

The duke instead remembered Carol very well. A month later Carol was officially invited by her aunt to introduce her to the duke of Essex. Carol didn't even remember him and almost refused to go. But Carol's aunt was very persuasive in telling Carol what a big catch he was and how much honor he would bring to the family's status. Little by little Carol let herself be seduced by the lure of power and fame. She thought that His grace was not a bad sort, he was a little bit older then she was, but he was charming. She thought to herself that he seems to be strong and understanding and she told herself, "Since I want to change many injustices in the world, by marrying this man I will have the opportunity and the money to do it." Carol would sometimes stay awake at night until the small hours of the morning dreaming of falling in love with this great man. Carol knew that the main reason why the duke was marrying her was because he wanted children to be heirs to his position and fortune. "I love children." Carol would say to herself so this is a plus not a minus. I will love my children with all my heart! She thought, and she would fall asleep smiling."

There were rumors about a lover and Carol pointedly asked the duke if it was true. He told her, "Nothing serious, Carol, nothing serious, there is nothing happening at all now." The duke hugged and kissed her and said, "I love you my beautiful Carol I could never betray you." During their betrothal the duke and Carol seldom went out alone. There was so much protocol to go by that they tried to stay close at home. Since the date of the marriage had been set and being always busy doing one thing or other in preparation for the wedding, time went by fast. Carol's picture was in all the newspapers of the world. Her beautiful face and smile was admired by thousands of people. It seemed that Carol was the daughter, the sister, the friend of everybody in the world.

People wanted to see how beautiful she looked. They wanted to see her grandiose wedding dress, veil, and shoes. The entourage was made up of the nobility not only of the city but also from the country at large. The necklace and the tiara were those of a queen. Carol was so beautiful and happy; she truly looked like a real queen. The day after the wedding, Carol and her noble husband left for their honeymoon. But they had very little privacy. Between the newspapers, the television and the paparazzi everybody was informed of whatever they did. Carol knew that she had to give up some of her privacy, but she did not know or even guess how much privacy she would no longer have. She didn't like it.

Carol at this stage was very busy trying to adjust to her new life. She felt like a hermit in a crowd because of the lack of privacy. Then she became pregnant and she was happy again. She was busy dreaming about her baby and preparing everything to the smallest detail. Carol liked to express herself freely and without reservations. Too often, the house staff and, in particular, her appointments secretary told her what to do. She decided and told everyone that she didn't believe in obeying all the dictates of the protocol of the house staff. She would do what she thought was right. Things had changed; there were too many vicissitudes. However, because the birth of the baby was forth coming, things improved a little. Then the baby was born. They named him Philip Stuart. Endless discussions and disagreements took place before and after the baby's birth because Carol wanted to breast feed the baby and spend a lot of time with him. The rules and protocol of the house were changed to give Carol the freedom she wanted in order to oversee her son's upbringing. Carol got pregnant again and this stopped the further deterioration of the situation for a time.

Then by chance, Carol found out that her husband had rekindled his affair with his mistress Lady Caroline Beltram. Carol immediately approached her husband who denied everything. Carol told him that if it was true she would divorce him. The Duke and the dowager, Lady Margaret, his mother had hard time accepting Carol's independent spirit. Nevertheless, they hoped that in time she would abide by the rules that were part of her life as a great Lady.

Carol was sure she could never become a follower, she wanted to help people. She wanted to alleviate the suffering of the poor and neglected. So she began to do something about it. She started visiting hospitals, especially children's hospitals, and nursing homes where she would sit by the beds of children, women, and men talking to them and comforting them. When she met with people she found some of them were victims of mines and unexploded bombs. The veterans and innocents of war were in her heart, in particular the ones that had been injured and maimed by those mines and bombs. She visited hospices and was never afraid or turned off when touching and hugging frail or very sick people. Whenever she arrived to see the victims of war, Carol brought hope and relief. By now she was known as the beautiful good lady. Her husband did not approve but Carol went her way just the same. After the birth of her second baby Carol stopped going around for a while because she wanted to raise the baby herself. Her second Baby was named Richard. She enjoyed being a mother and tried to do the best she could as she was stressed by the conflicts that were going on at home. The Duke, Carol's husband, had publicly been seen with Lady Beltram. His grace could no longer deny his affair with her to Carol. Carol did not accept this and would not have anything to do with her husband and so from one month to another this state of things continued quickly deteriorating. Carol became a prey for the paparazzi that followed her everywhere. Simple friendship with important men was reported as love affairs, anything that Carol did was big news. His Grace, her husband, wasn't helping at all as he continued his love affair with Lady Caroline Beltram. As things were not getting any better, Jerome and Carol decided to file for divorce and in less than a year, the noble couple was divorced.

Carol after almost 12 years was free and in charge of herself. After a few years, Carol met and fell in love with a very handsome and charming man. He was from Morocco and a commoner. He was not poor. Actually, he was the son of a millionaire. His family owned a chain of high fashion stores. His name was Moshad Namir. The Namiri fashion stores were famous in all Europe and even in the Americas and could afford to live in luxury. Mr. Namiri, Moshad's father, was an imposing good-looking man with a dark completion, black hair and black eyes. He was against Carol and his son's relationship. He knew the danger and was afraid for his son's safety but in the end he had to accept things as they were. Carol and Moshad were together always; they truly loved each other and decided to get married. That was a true bombshell. If Carol married a commoner and had children, their children would become step brothers or sisters of the Duke's children and that was not possible. Someone must do something. But what could be done? Short of killing her, Jerome could not think of any other way. He thought about it for a while and then he decided to talk with his mother who is the great Ann Kingsley. The radical conduct of Carol completely outraged the Lady Ann. She told her son that yes he must do something to put an end to her reproachable behavior for the sake of the children. She said to her son that they should have a secret family meeting to see what they could do together. The lady Ann was a tall very skinny woman, she had black eyes and brown hair, a large mouth with thin lips, every day she wore different ostentatiously rich dresses and necklaces. She made her authority felt by all that dealt with her. She asked her son to invite his mistress Lady Bertram and two other loyal members of the family to the meeting. Lady Ann opened the meeting. "This secret family meeting has been convened to discuss and take action regarding the scandalous behavior of Carol Stanton. It is imperative that we stop her marriage with the commoner Moshad Namiri. I suggest that each one of us write on a piece of paper the best way to stop her outrageous behavior." Lady Beltram asked "Shouldn't we discuss it before we write?" "No!" answered the dowager, "it is better that is secret. We put our scrap of paper in a box then we will see what we have written and if we all agree, we will each put a blank white paper in the box except me. I will put the written one back in the box. We will draw papers. The person that gets the written paper will do the job. He or she will use whatever means is necessary. If you agree with me about how this meeting will decide what to do, raise your hand." Lady Ann raised her hand and all the others followed. Lady Ann said, "I see we all agree."

Lady Ann then distributed a folded paper to each family member present. After they had all written their solution to the problem on their paper and refolded it, each one of them placed their folded paper in the box. Lady Ann took each paper out and read the proposed solution. She then said, "It seems that everyone agrees on the solution, so I will put the last folded paper into the box along with a blank folded sheet for each of you. After the papers were in the box, each family member drew out a folded paper. Lady Ann asked, "Will the person with the written solution please raise their hand?" After someone raised their hand, Lady Ann asked everyone to take note of who is responsible.

Lady Ann continued, "Now since we will all be equally responsible for this terrible deed, we have to know who will do the job so that we can help if necessary while he or she is doing the job. We cannot be too open about discussing this problem, even now, someone can be listening to us, so please burn you paper and get on to solving this horrible problem. I adjourn this meeting. From now on, we will call the person that drew the card Lady X.

Lady X was elated - yes, she would solve the problem. Nevertheless, she was not very happy about having drawn the paper with the solution. She would do her best to accomplish the job because her hatred of Carol was so great. But where should she start? Sure, she could go to the assassination bureau but too many people would know and it would not be wise. She had to think and think hard. Then like a flash, she remembered that the son of her housekeeper worked at the Namiri Main store as a guard. She had to find out everything she could about the family and kind of people they were to make sure that Lady Carol was going to be eliminated if she really wanted to marry in this family of rich commoners. As time passed, Lady X gathered a lot of information and got to know who were the personal guards, of Moshad and Lady Carol, the bodyguards' families and friends and after a long selection of people, she finally found a weak link she could trust.

Justin Welsh was a well renowned lawyer. He had the best clientele in the city of Lancashire a large city in the suburbs of mount Stanislaus. In the last decade, the small town of Lancashire had become a large prosperous city due to a well-known Casino that employed over one thousand employees. The Law firm of Justin Welsh had the casino as his biggest client. The firm employed 10 lawyers and 5 administrative employees and was doing very well.

Justin Welsh during his younger years had been a suspect of his girlfriend's murder. He avoided jail because the son of Mrs. X's housekeeper had provided an impeccable fake alibi. He was cleared of all charges and went home free. Mrs. Robin Reese, Mrs. X's housekeeper, did not know anything about the murder of Justin Welsh's girlfriend, she knew that at the time of the murder her son and Justin Welsh were together and that because of her son's testimony Justin was acquitted. Mrs. X knew of the trial and the involvement of her housekeeper's son and wanted to know more about it. She, under a fictitious name, hired a private investigator to find out if there was any doubt about Justin Welsh's innocence. The investigator found out that at the time of the murder of Justin Welsh's girlfriend, the housekeeper's son was out of Town. Lady X didn't waste any time and after getting the report from the private investigator invited her housekeeper to lunch in her private garden. As they sat at a table in the garden Lady X came immediately to the point. "Robin I am afraid I have bad news for you, regarding your son. Your son committed perjury during a murder trial." Robin jumped up, but Lady X, while she lifted her hand, said "please don't worry I am not going to turn him in to the police, but I need a big favor from you." Her housekeeper answered, "Sure my lady anything that I can do for you I will be happy to do." Lady X said, "This is a very big and dangerous thing and only you can help me. There is no right way to say it; so I have to tell you that I need to have someone killed." Her housekeeper replied, "Oh my lady! I don't know what to say." Lady X said, "Say yes. Robin you only can say yes or your son is going to jail, now calm down and I tell you who we have to kill." The housekeeper meekly questioned, "Who my lady, who?" After a small hesitation Lady X said, "The Lady Carol, Robin. She will marry a commoner. She, this time has gone too far. We cannot allow his grace's children to become step brothers with the children of a commoner." The housekeeper replied, "My lady couldn't another way be found? What happens if someone discovers our plot?" Lady X said, "Our actions will not be discovered Robin. Your son is a very smart guy, I know that he has many people he can trust, but in this case he cannot trust anyone – not even his friends." answered Lady X. "Things have got to be worked out to perfection no one should ever know the truth. Naturally, the death must be accidental. As lady Carol travels with her boyfriend extensively there will be many chances to do the job, your son is a great mechanic and he already works there he has got to fix a car so that it will breakdown without raising suspicion. Talk to your son Robin, I am sure he will know what to do then let me know, We will have lunch here again next week I will let you know when," Lady X finished. Robin was very worried, her gut feeling was presaging problems, she knew that for her and her son there was no way out of this terrible thing and she began to weep. The next day she requested an audience with Lady X. When she met with Lady X, she requested and Lady X gave her a week vacation to spend with her son. She did not ask for anything else. Lady X shook Robin's hand and said,

"Have a good time Robin, I count on you." "Thank you my lady. I will. You can count on me," answered Robin as she left.

Robin's son Alan Reese was a very good-looking man. He was thirty five years old. He was athletic and very charming, he was the typical achiever. He liked to mix with rich people so he dressed well, but had a big passion for cars in general and spent a lot of time caring for the cars and driving the car. He once made a wager saying that he could disassemble a car build it back again in less than three days. He won the wager and from that day on he was called the smart mechanic. He prided himself on having friends in high places or, better, having friends that worked for people in high places. In fact, Stanley Cammon and Fred Butler, who were his best friends, worked as bodyguards for the son of the millionaire of the Namiri fashion chain stores. Moshad Namiri, who at the time was engaged with Carol Stanton, was looking for expert drivers. Immediately after Alan Reese spoke with his mother, he invited his friends to dinner. He had a good time with them and asked them if their boss needed a driver, as he liked to drive instead of working as a guard. Moshad knew Alan to be a good driver and a good mechanic, so he was happy to hire him as his personal driver. After working as a driver for a year Alan was so good in his job that he was made Moshad's and Carol's personal driver. He had shown them such devotion that they treated him more as a friend than as an employee. Moshad loved to run with him, go to long rides asking advice on how to change a tire and take care of a car in general. Alan's knowledge and confidence impressed Moshad. When Alan drove a car - any car, it seemed that the car became alive in his hands.

Moshad and Alan had many rallies together and though Alan won all the time Moshad didn't get hurt and respected Alan for his genius to get the most out of a car. After few Months Alan had became for the Namiri Family the most trusted driver. Moshad and Carol decided to go to France for a two week vacation because Carol wanted to buy her trousseau in France. The trip was planned very carefully. They would go by car. The couple was to be accompanied by two body-guards and by Alan who would drive the car. All five people were happy and wanted to have a splendid trip. Alan worked very hard to prepare the car chosen for the trip. He prepared the car so that at the right moment he could crash the car. Alan hated himself for what he had agreed to do. He really liked Carol and Moshad, but he felt very bad for his friends above all. He loved life but he could not see himself going on with his life after what he had prepared to do. He did it to please his mother and save her life. Because he knew that if he didn't do it, someone would kill him and his mother. No one who dared to displease the mighty rich nobles lived to tell about it. He felt the uttermost disgust for all of them. Above all, he hated Lady X. There was very little chance, but if he lived through the ordeal, he would kill her. He hated her so much that he dreamed of strangling her and then jumping up and down on her dead body.

Alan had one problem; Carol should not wear a seat

belt so that the impact would throw her forword and upward. She would hit her head against the ceiling of the car. For the others he did worry the impact would be so strong that no one would survive. He broke the rear seat belt fastener so that it would not latch closed. Moshad gave to Carol a large bouquet of flowers. Alan, as eager to please as always, asked "My Lady may I put the flowers in the back seat beside you?" Carol replied, "Yes, Alan, thank you," and she entered the car. After everybody was in the car, Alan started the car. Everybody was happy and everyone was telling jokes, laughing, and having a good time. Alan for the first time in his life was nervous at the wheel, he wanted to scream all of you get out, there is still time to save yourselves, but his mouth remained shut tight and he could not utter a word. As the chosen place loomed ahead in the distance, he felt faint. He struggled with himself and then screamed - out everybody out, but it was too late. The last thing that Alan remembered was Carol looking at him with horror, but it was too late.

Nevertheless, Alan did not die in the car as he wished. When he woke up in the hospital, he realized that he had survived. He had survived because he wore his seat belt, but neither of the people he was driving had survived because they did not wear their seat belts. After the accident Alan was never the same as before. He drank to forget and became an unreliable driver. Because he was so unreliable, he never had any steady work or famous clients again.

The C P C of the Bay
Area Mail Nightmare

*T*he cerebral Palsy center of the bay area found its place in the heart of the Oakland hills. The location is ideal. Built on a rocky hillside, the center has an aura of solidity and strength. The city of Oakland lies beneath a spacious green backyard, which offers a beautiful view of the bay area and surrounding cities. At midday, when the sun's rays strike and reflect off the waters of the bay, the center becomes a platform of sparkles and lights. At the entrance, the parking lot nestled at the bottom of a steep hill which almost is completely covered with trees and bushes. Most of the trees are tall and very beautiful, but some of the bushes fight to take nourishment from the very rocky slope. At the center of the hill a large pyracantha bush blooms throughout the winter, showing its red berries, creating a joyful atmosphere of festivity and life. The constant gentle breeze shuffling through the leaves is a reminder to the onlooker of the world's continuous motion.

At the top of the hill, the Greek Orthodox Church of the Ascension stands in a lovely setting of strikingly beautiful trees and bushes including many olive and juniper trees. On the left side of the front landscape, near Lincoln Avenue, there is a large shallow pond with a few dark red and brown fish overlooking the bay.

The structure seems like any other Greek Orthodox Church from the outside. However, as I enter, the ornamental ceiling hits me with inspiration. The first look strikes me with dark brown luminosity showing a combination of strong red, blue, and green colors. Then my eyes are drawn to the center of the ceiling where the patient lovely face of Jesus gives me a wonderful feeling of peace and unity which spreads all though me and brings tears to my eyes. The apostles surround Jesus looking contentedly up to him. He seems to have a message of hope for whoever chooses to look to him. And to remind them to be happy for their sacrifice because he said that those who helped the poor and the helpless would gain entrance to heaven and enjoy eternal life. Happiness radiates from the ceiling to all who look up to see it.

On the south side of the CP center, a few well kept houses peek out above the bushes and trees. The houses seem to be searching for sunlight. At the very top of the hill rises the Mormon Temple with its five golden spires. It seems to keep a watchful eye on the Center and its clients. Between the CPC and the Mormon temple there is a very close relationship. The people that come to participate in special activities use their parking lot without charge. The clients love the special activities that happen on these occasions, they love to talk and laugh with everybody. The CP Center rises above the bushes and trees, as if searching for light. The CP center has an enchanting view with a superb panorama of the bay, the bridges, and the cities. It seems to separate the churches and the CP center from the everyday life in the cities below them. Looking down from the CP Center, the view of the city of Oakland and the surrounding bay area is simply enchanting. A superb panorama of the bay, the bridges, and the various cities is a spectacle that delights the eyes.

Among these surroundings the CP Center helps to serve the needs of its clients in any way that it can. It strives to make the clients a part of the everyday life that they desire. The clients, relatives, parents, and staff and volunteers meet every week to find ways to make the clients life better. Since I began to work for the cerebral palsy center, I have met many volunteers whom I admire and value very much. My big encounter with this army of loving soldiers occurred when the center found itself with 250,000 pieces of mail to be manually postage stamped and mailed. A mistake had been made and all the 250,000 pieces of mail had been returned by the Post Office. There was nothing else to do but correct the error and ship all the 250,000 pieces of mail back. After the news we were all in uproar because 250,000 pieces of mail had to be redone. It was the biggest fund raising effort of the year. It was very important that the job be done within four days or the forthcoming carousel capers fair would be jeopardized. From that moment on everybody got busy. Phone calls were made asking for help. Flyers were made and distributed all around the area by volunteers who manually took them by car or bus.

Before the day was out many people knew and started coming to the center to help. They came and worked very hard till late at night. It made everyone proud to see the volunteers when they worked, played, laughed, and sacrificed to help others. At the CPC center we have another special group of volunteers. They are the mothers of the clients. They come to volunteer on a regular basis. Some volunteer on Mondays only because on the other weekdays, they work; while other volunteers are here every day. These tireless workers do so much for the center. What a beautiful message of love they send to all with their earnest and generous giving; they add a new dimension to the never surpassed beauty of maternal love. With their help the center helps the sick and the needy; they want it to grow, so that their children, who are especially close to their hearts, can have a place where they can find care and love. As I mentioned before the previous week volunteers and staff for a week worked to complete an important mailing. At the end we were very tired and very happy. We had completed the mailing in record time. Mrs. Mary Ross, the director of the center, is a very good cook and she had promised all of us a good dinner and a lovely party.

The food and the party were excellent; we were very happy and proud of ourselves.

However, three days later word came from the post office that the large mailing, all of the 250,000 pieces would be returned because of an error in the address code and a small difference in weight. All the letters must be corrected within four days. On the day that the post office sent the mail back, the director restarted the mailing again. A meeting was scheduled for the next day. Flyers were sent, telephone calls were made to inform everybody of the problem, and to request help again. People came in droves. All were concerned and eager to help.

For four days, we worked hard all day and into the night to re-stamp each of the 250,000 envelopes. Volunteers of all ages showed up whenever they could. Some came after work, some before or after supper, some that did not have to go to work came to help all day. I looked at their smiling faces with delight. Not even a big sporting event that was going on at the time could keep the volunteers at home and away from where they were needed. It was beautiful. The volunteers at work made me think of God and harmony.

On the third night, I was in a room with Thomas Weadon and his wife Mariana at my table and a young couple with a thick accent. They had a sick child at the center they cared for him very much. They worked very hard for his welfare. The child was still very young and the mother would stop working now and then to go to check up on him. I have to confess that I was touched.

The room was filled with stacks of letters we had already stamped. It was a warm night, the windows and doors were open. Outside it was very dark and very quiet.

Down the hill, the city seemed to be dormant and without troubles. The lights shining in the night added to this beautiful picture an aura of warmth and mystery that induced one to dream and see a world of love and peace. Once in awhile the chirp of a cricket could be heard and it sounded like a prayer to God. I asked myself could this be true or become true? I certainly I hope so! Just then a sense of euphoria pervaded me. For a moment, I was happy really happy. I awoke from this beautiful trance by the screeching of tires on the road below. A truck had just arrived. It was filled with more sacks of unstamped letters. It was immediately emptied and refilled with more stamped envelopes. We were working as fast as we possibly we could, we were aware of the big task still ahead of us. It was almost 10:30 P M. After repeatedly and rapidly sticking postage stamps, we were growing very weary.

Just then we opened the next sack of unstamped letters, and a bit of comic relief arrived to amuse us. I don't know who started it, but someone said, "After sticking on so many stamps, I can see those stamps sprouting wings!" A voice was heard. A loud general laugh ensued. From that moment on, not only were we stamping envelopes, but we were also creating a monster stamp. It became a game, so in a very short time, each of us in turn had created and attached a limb to this ever growing postage stamp. Each one of us contributed to the stamp and added each part of his enormous body. I have to admit that by imagining this monster stamp, as the saying goes, we went a bit overboard. The monster was tall and large. His head was like a pyramid. A long nose sprang out of his head like a folded accordion and ended with his nostril folded upward. The eyes were large round and dark blue, but the eyebrows were braided and tied behind his head in a sloppy knot. Long green hair fell from the top of the head, while the beard was whirls of curly blue hairs. The blue eyes shed a continuous stream of tears, the mouth with full lips was always moving emitting gibberish and at times strange sounds that could have been swear words. Most of us were laughing loudly. So it seemed that every time he saw us laugh, he would motion menacingly as if an attack was beginning. Every time he uttered a word, bubbles would froth from the gaps of his yellowish, crooked teeth. His checks were puffy and red but his neck was thin long and wrinkled. His ears were like an indoor UHF antenna: large round rings pushed out from his face. Despite his short spindly arms his legs were disproportionately long and thin, his feet were short, his toes long and similar to the claws of chickens; yet his hands were large covered with purple hair, while his fingers were long and had no nails. He wore red and blue striped pants and a tight red pink top. He had no shoes and no hat at that very moment.

I even thought it was close to midnight a shipment of envelopes was ready to go to the post office, and when almost all of us tried to hand out the sacks full of mail to the postman we heard a voice scream in terror "Watch out! The monster stamp is coming to get you. Absolute silence followed the scream then a roar of laughter followed. We then moved all the tables and furniture against the walls and we went to the center of the very large room where we joined hands, formed a circle, and began to sing and dance with red faces and big smiles. I believe that at that moment we experienced true happiness. When we were ready to walk out of the room someone screamed, "Hey! Don't forget that the director will treat us to one of her delicious dinners. She also said that she will invite all the people that came to help. Hurrah!"

The Infamous Bridge Gallina

*I*t *was nine o'clock in* the morning and the sad and prolonged tolls of the church's bells abruptly suspended the usual noises of the city. "Oh! God another one jumped at the bridge Gallina. Who is this time?" everybody would say in the city. All the activities of the moment were suspended: mothers, fathers, sisters, brothers and all concerned who could not account for their relatives were making sure that their loved ones were at the places they were supposed to be. All this would happen when four tolls of the church bells sounded in the air to announce a suicide. People would run to the police station to find out who had jumped this time. The landscape of the outskirts of the city of Tiliape in its wild, almost deserted plateau is quite impressive. Few skeletal trees and large bushes populate an area of about two kilometers wide and four kilometers in length. This area is divided in the middle by the river gallina (hen). The river is very deep and water runs abundantly in winter but in summer it becomes almost a trickle.

The origin of the name of the river is unknown, When viewing the river by any side there is nothing that suggest such a name: There is a legend which says that a very poor woman living in the near city of Tiliape used to bring chickens to feed on the right bank of the river. One day one of her hens went too close to the edge of the river and stood on a stone. The stone fell, under the weight of the hen, in the river taking the hen with it into the water. The woman tried but could not save her hen which drowned. When she arrived back in town, the woman went to all her neighbors recounting the incident and begging for a replacement as the eggs that her Hen (gallina) produced were her only income. No one gave her a hen or any help and she went on crying for weeks about her hen. People would ridicule her, singing "poor Clara lost her riches in the river, what did she loose? She lost her best and productive gallina." From that day on the name of the river became gallina. On the river there was a bridge that was used by the farmers to go cross to the other side to sell or exchange merchandise in the towns between the two sides of the river.

During the winter there wasn't much traffic because the bridge was in disrepair and the iced snow stayed for a long time and few, if any, people ventured to pass by it. During the summer; because the river was very deep the traffic increased but not very much because people were afraid to fall, in fact, no one dared look below the bridge because the bridge was so tall and too many people experienced vertigo. At times, the donkeys that were used to transport the farmers' wares refused to cross the bridge. Bridge gallina was not a very popular bridge.

In town, Mr. Cosimo Capitelli, a very rich land owner, was a very handsome man. He was tall and dark. He had black hair, eyes, and was well mannered and smart. He, with his wife and children lived in a large beautiful house surrounded by three acres of land. His gardener, Giulio Baratti, was not rich but was very handsome. He could write, read, and play the violin very well. He kept the outside of the place beautifully, grew the family vegetable and lots of flowers. Giulio had a girlfriend, Filomena, who was of extraordinary beauty. Filomena's parents had great hopes for her because of her beauty. They did not want their daughter to associate herself with a gardener. They, therefore, refused to give Giulio their daughter's hand in marriage and thus they didn't want to receive him in their house. Filomena and Giulio met when they could, and they met often in the garden of Mr. Cosimo Capitelli. They were very discrete but soon enough Mr. Capitelli saw them making love, he did not say anything to Giulio but waited for Filomena the next day before she reached the garden. He stopped her and told her that he had seen her with Giulio and that he would have to fire Giulio and report her to her parents. Filomena got very scared and fell on her knees and said "Oh, please Mr. Capitelli don't tell my parents My parents will kill me and Giulio will lose his job, he has an old mother that is very poor she will starve without Giulio 's help." Mr. Capitelli took Filomena by her hands and, while helping her up, he took her in his arms saying:" OK, Filomena I will help you but you have to be nice to me. Come tomorrow morning to my office and we will take care of things." Filomena knew the kind of help Mr. Capitelli would give her, or better, the price she would have to pay for his help. The day after Filomena was worried and she tried to find the right words to say to Mr. Capitelli. She had a bad feeling of foreboding.

A few times she turned back to return home, she was determined not to go, but she thought of the consequences for Giulio and his family. In the end, she decided to go and beg her way out of any disgraceful thing that Mr. Capitelli may want her to do. Surely if she said no it would be no, he could not force her to do anything she did not want to do. After all, Giulio could find another job. So, Filomena reassured by these thoughts presented herself to Mr. Capitelli's office. Mr. Capitelli was very elegant; he invited Filomena to sit down, offered her wine and told her that she was very beautiful and that he loved her.

"Mr. Capitelli, I pray you to listen to me. I am not a bad girl. I let Giulio make love to me because I love him. And I will never do anything that could jeopardize our happiness. You are a married man and your wife will be very mad at you when she finds out that you invited me here. I told my parents about Giulio," continued Filomena, "and I convinced them that I love him, and that I can only be happy, if I marry him. At the beginning of the discussion, my parents didn't like the idea of me marrying Giulio, but now they are OK with it.

So, if you please, you can tell them since they will not punish me." At this point Mr. Capitelli threw himself on Filomena, shut her mouth with his mouth and proceeded to rape her. Philomena taken by surprise did not have time to defend herself and was brutally raped. While being raped Filomena fought with all her might, kicking, biting, scratching, and screaming. She savagely scratched his left cheek making him bleed. Afterwards Mr.Capitelli repeatedly hit her and then threw her out of his office. People had heard Filomena's screams and had come to the office building. As she left the office, Filomena cried "he raped me, Mr. Capitelli raped me" while tears were flowing from her eyes. Of the people gathered in front of Mr. Capitelli's office, a few tried to comfort Filomena; but no one showed any indignation toward the vile, cruel act that Mr. Capitelli committed against her.

All of the people outside the office retreated to where they came from. They were afraid of the consequences that would follow if they eased Filomena's pain and suffering. Mr. Capitelli was their boss so they feared for their jobs. Mr. Capitelli's wife, Nancy, hearing the commotion ran into his office where her husband told her that Filomena had attacked him because he refused to give Giulio a raise to marry her. Nancy Capitelli was a short and very plump woman with a gray unkempt head of hair. She envied Filomena for her beauty and could not forgive her for attacking her husband, even if in her heart, she knew that her husband was lying. Mrs. Capitelli was known for her nasty disposition. She came out of his office screaming at Filomena. She called her a whore and told her not to ever set foot on the premises again. The office called a doctor to take care of Mr. Capitelli, whose cheek was badly damaged and bleeding.

Mr. Capitelli immediately fired Giulio. Giulio believed that Filomena was innocent, but because she had gone into Mr. Capitelli's office without telling him about her previous encounter with Mr. Capatelli and because she went in his office alone, he felt that he could not marry Filomena anymore. He told her how sorry he was but that he could not love her anymore. "Giulio", answered Filomena, "I thought that Mr. Capitelli was an honest man. I never imagined that he could be so mean, so brutal. I am innocent! Giulio, I love you. How can you leave me when you know that I am innocent?" He replied, "Filomena, I cannot marry you, I would be the talk of the town if I did. As it is I have to find another job, goodbye and don't come after me. "He left without looking at her. Filomena's parents were very upset for what had happened and for her sleeping around with Giulio before getting married. From that day on they were less friendly with her, especially after Filomena was fired from her job because of the incident with Mr. Capitelli. The Town's people shamed her; she had became a pariah. When the scandal had quieted down a little, Filomena could, at times, find work as a maid, but her life was very hard. The women were afraid of her and the men were too friendly which was more offensive then the women's fear. Life was truly unbearable for

Filomena and often she found herself praying to God to let her die. Then the worst happened! Filomena found out that she was pregnant; she did not dare tell her parents or anyone else. She knew that her parents would cast her out of the house and that she would lose her work, as bad as it would be, too. After one night staying awake and thinking, she remembered a woman that for a fee would get rid of an unwanted pregnancy. Her name was Viola Sutter. Viola was a farm worker, when young she had worked in a hospital as a nurse aide, She was still young about 45/50 years old, she had a pleasant personality, she lived alone in a small cottage that she had inherited from her parents, she was known to be: discrete and that she didn't ask questions.

Filomena after thinking a long time about it decided to go to see Viola even though it was very painful. She equated abortion to killing. Under normal conditions she would have been very happy to have a child. Now her heart was sad and her eyes would well up with tears at the thought of ridding herself of her baby. She loved him or her and was terrified at the thought that he was growing and that she would have to kill him. Filomena did not have enough money to pay to have the abortion done immediately; she had to wait two more months to have enough money to pay Viola.

At almost four Months the fetus was big and Filomena suffered immensely during the procedure. She felt that the best part of her life had died. Afterwards a little bloody form of a baby was presented to her. The poor fetus was badly cut up; parts of limbs were separated from the not identifiable bleeding form. Filomena was shaking and crying desperately she got the little bundle in her arms, she didn't know what to do where to go or who to ask for help. So in a panic she began to run.

She ran and ran while the little bundle became redder and redder. After a while she heard the sound of running water, she ran towards the water and found herself on the Gallina Bridge, she stopped. Thinking that she would wash the baby, she opened the bundle and saw the little head which was less bloody now but still horribly deformed, she knew that she would never be able to survive the horror of what had happened and decided to jump over the bridge with her baby.

She was bitter and very unhappy. No one helped her, no one would help her. She was alone and desperate. She found herself wanting revenge; she wanted to punish the people that had brought her to this desperate and painful state. After all she was innocent, and they had to pay.

She laid the little bundle on the bridge. She fell on her knees. Then she said while lifting her hands to the sky, "I, Filomena Ventura, curse all the people that brought me to this point in my life. Those people should come to this bridge and kill themselves as I now am killing myself out of desperation. I curse you and your descendants for all of the generations to come." She got the little bloody bundle and put it to her breast, under her dress near to her heart. Then she jumped off the bridge. After a week her body; horribly broken up, was found. Though they tried, no one could move her hands from her chest. So she was buried as she was found.

The only people that showed up for her funeral were her parents and Giulio. All of them repented the cruelty they showed her and cried about the loss of their beautiful unfortunate girl. One year later Filomena's curse, for the first time, came to pass. Mr. Capitelli was found at the bottom of the bridge Gallina with his body as broken up as Filomena's body was. Mrs. Capitelli, who had never believed her in husband's remorse for Filomena's death, was surprised when the remorse drove her husband to jump off the bridge. To this day very mad or angry people continue to say, "I cannot take it anymore! I am going to jump from the Bridge to end my misery. Not all the people that threaten to jump really jump, but many people, thru the years, have jumped. People jump, to this day, off the Gallina Bridge out of desperation and die.

The Saint of Paterson

*T**he children of the Romano** family were very excited, all the ten of them. Everybody was, all at once, trying to put their things in order, and they created pandemonium; they were screaming, running, and telling one another what to do. Their aunt, who played the nanny for all of them, was very busy trying to shelter the very young from the fury of the older ones who were running around like crazy. Their ruckus tore the rooms apart. All this was happening because; News had reached the family that the mother of the famous Saint of Paterson would come to visit them. Every year she would pay a visit to them bringing a lot of fresh fruits, vegetables and sweet cakes, her name was Mrs. Annina Figone. She was a simple gentle woman and the children loved her. Annina Figone was very thin, of medium height. She had big brown eyes, and at the age of 45 her air was almost all grey, she still wore the costume of the early thirties that was very interesting and beautiful. It was composed of three pieces: A pleated skirt, a multicolored apron and a top with pleats on both sides and a row of buttons in the front. The costume top was trimmed with lace at the neckline. As it was the custom, she wore a large scarf on her head anytime that she went out for any reason. These scarves were made of silk. They were very ornate with beautiful designs, her hands though long and thin showed the sign of hard work in the fields and at home.

At that time the very large Romano family was on vacation in the mountains. Every year after the school year ended, the parents would reluctantly send their children to the mountains for the fresh air and relaxation. When the family was together, there was no way they could do any work. Mr. and Mrs. Patel Romano both worked in their store and were out of their home from eight o' clock in the morning to nine o' clock at night during the summer vacation they got together with their children and two aunts that took care of them during the weekend. The children were happy to be in the mountains because they usually had fewer chores to do and many hours of the day to play. In the town where this big family lived there was a custom that when a couple had a child, the child had to have a padrino (Godfather) if he was a boy, or a madrina (Godmother) if she was a girl. The first child of the Romano family had been a boy, so he became a padrino when he was an adult. Annina's daughter was named Tonia. When Tonia was a grown woman, she became the Saint of Patherson.

The two families exchanged presents once or twice a year; Mrs. Figone usually came during the summer because she loved to see the children all together. She lived with her family in Patherson. Patherson was a rural village very close to the town of Licari where the Romano family lived. The village had a few houses, and some cultivated land for goats and sheep to graze surrounded the houses. Everybody kept chickens and other small animals around their houses. The market for all the surrounding area was here. Almost all the people of Licari bought their vegetables, milk, eggs, and chickens to sell or trade here on market days.

That day after supper the children asked Mrs. Figone if she would tell them something about Tonia her saintly and now famous daughter. Mrs. Figone gladly acquiesced to their request and went outside with them, to their very large and long porch. The beautiful valley below could be admired from there. It was a beautiful night. The moon was high and brilliant in the sky. The stars; luminous and plentiful covered the full area above them. They sat in circle around Mrs. Figone. All around there was' an atmosphere of expectation and wonder, even the youngest children that habitually were always in motion were quiet and attentively waiting for Mrs. Figone to begin to talk.

Mrs. Figone with her serene smiling face began to tell her story. "Since the very day I bore my daughter, Tonia," Mrs. Figone said, "I could tell that she was a special child. My husband and I could see that the child was different. While all the rest of the family had darkish complexion, Tonia looked like an angel. She had long blond hair, blue eyes, and a very fair complexion. Since she opened her eyes for the first time, she kept her eyes open with a smiling face. It looked like she was watching all of us, one by one, in the eyes. We found it a little strange, my husband especially, kept looking at her and at me with a strange expression; to tell you the truth, I began to worry. However, thank God, Tonia had a birth mark common to my husband's side of the family. It was a little red mole on the back of the left ear. This discovery put my husband at ease and the two of us had a good laugh about it. Tonia was so easy to raise she hardly ever cried. While growing up she was obedient and very good at any task that she performed. She loved to pray and go to church; she would dance at the sound of the bells calling the people to Mass. We really thought that she would become a nun. But that wasn't God's will. Tonia, even though she was modest, always was attracted to boys. Gianni, The son of our next door neighbor was the boy that she liked the most. Gianni was very handsome. He was of medium height, thin, a hard worker in the field, and a good shepherd. We loved him, soon enough our families became closer, and it was understood that both Gianni and Tonia would one day get married."

When Tonia was sixteen years old she became thoughtful, she didn't talk very much, and she was pensive like she was in a trance all day long. Worried, I asked her if there was something wrong, she didn't answer immediately; but after a while she fell on her knees and started crying '"Oh mamma," she said, "I think I am crazy." "But why? Tonia, what makes you think so? You cannot be crazy, you do everything so well and you are so beautiful. Please tell me what makes you think such horrible thing,' I replied. "Oh Mamma you will not believe me if I tell you," Tonia said. I replied, "Oh, but I will my daughter, I will, I know you too well to doubt you, please tell me." Tonia, shaking a little, said, "you see mother, I see things and I hear things: I hear animals talk, I see people that no one else sees, and the birds sing with a human voice to me, I sometimes talk to them too." I was speechless for a while but then I thought how good she was and how different she was from all of us; so, taking her in my arms like when she was a baby, I told her, 'Tonia, my dear child, I don't think that you are crazy. I think that God is telling you that you belong to him." "But mamma," answered Tonia "How this can be? I have feelings for Gianni. I think I want to marry him, but if this is God's will, as you believe, I am ready to become a nun. I love Gianni but I love God more." She was subdued when I said, "listen child, let us do this. We will kneel and pray God to give us a sign to know his will." Afterwards, we both felt better and resumed our usual chores. The same day, as was the custom of the town, Gianni accompanied by his parents came to our house to ask Mr. and Mrs. Figone for Tonia's hand in marriage to Gianni. My husband and I were closed mouth for few minutes before answering. We had, previously talked about what to say if Gianni's parents asked for the hand of Tonia for their Gianni.

We were still at loss about how to answer them. Could we tell them that Tonia listened to animals' talking and that she talked back to them? Could we tell them that Tonia could see and hear what no one saw or heard? We wanted to answer their question, but we didn't know what to say because we were afraid that Tonia might be ridiculed and it would break Tonia's heart knowing how much she loved Gianni. Although we believed Tonia, at times we had doubts and we told Gianni's parents that we had to think about it and would give an answer to them very soon. Gianni's parents were a little disappointed the day after, because they thought that was understood that Gianni and Tonia would marry. Both my husband and I, again, fell on our knees and prayed God to show us a sign that he approved the marriage. That same night the sewing machine started to sew by itself all night. The sound of the machine awoke us. We tried to stop the machine but we could not. Then a wonderful scent of clean sheets permeated the room. My husband and I hugged each other and exclaimed, "The sign, this is the sign we asked God to give us to believe our daughter." We went to visit Gianni's parents on the next day. We told them, "The fact that we had not accepted the marriage proposal immediately had created a cold atmosphere of surprise and resentment between the two families, but we needed to think about it, so we decided to tell them everything and ask for their forgiveness afterwards." Mr. and Mrs. Scalisi, Gianni's parents, changed their attitude as soon as they heard both our reasons for our reluctance and our request for their forgiveness for not immediately accepting their request. Both of our families were very happy. Immediately, the atmosphere cleared and we called over the two young lovers who, very nervous, were waiting in the anteroom. In a moment all of us were embracing and kissing. The room was, now, full of relatives and friends congratulating the two young people, singing songs, and drinking wine. After three months, the young lovers were betrothed. The betrothal festivities lasted until the small hours on the next day.

"The happiest of the bunch with the exception of Tonia and Gianni were Mr. and Mrs. Scalisi who loved Tonia like a true daughter. Mrs. Scalisi was a sturdy and strong woman. She was a mother of six children, 5 boys and a girl that she loved greatly. She adored the girl, who was her last child, so she doted upon her. Mrs. Scalisi had a fair complexion, green eyes and blondish hair. She laughed a lot, hugged and kissed everyone that she met, no matter of which gender, she was a happy soul and was always trying to make everybody else happy. Mr. Scalisi, on the other hand, was a rude short man. He wore eyeglasses because of an injury to his right eye that happened when he was a soldier in World War II. He loved his farm and spent most of his time working in it. He worked rain or shine."

Mrs. Figone continued her story. "He too loved his little girl with all his heart. Before the marriage Tonia invited Gianni to walk to church to make sure everything was in order for the ceremony. On their way to the church, they found a vacant bench and Tonia invited

Gianni to sit nearby her. After sitting down, Tonia, blushing, took Gianni's hands in hers. She told him, 'Gianni you know how much I love you, please don't interrupt me. I have something very important to tell you before we get married. I should have told you before but I was afraid I could lose you.' At this point, Gianni became very pale and started shaking. 'Oh Gianni! I am a virgin. I assure you that no man has ever touched me. It is about another matter that I want to talk you.' He quickly replied, 'Anything my love, tell me anything, I assure you, nothing can keep me away from you. For a moment I was scared, but not even what I thought you were telling could keep me away from you. I love you too much.' My daughter said, 'Thank you, Gianni. I was scared too. You know Gianni that I am a little bit different. Since I was a young girl, I have understood the talk of animals and I have answered them back. I, also, see dead people and talk to them, I can see the future and the past of all the people that ask me. If this is too much for you to bear, I will not blame you for leaving me Gianni.' Gianni quickly asserted, 'Leave you? Never, my love, never! You know what? Now that I think of it, I will help you do all the good you can to the people that ask you for help, what you have is a gift of God not a disgrace. I have always felt that you were different. Your goodness and grace is not human, it comes from God. We will work together into this new phase of our lives. I have always dreamed of you dressed in white with a crown of flowers on your head. Because I was dreaming the same dream so, at times, it puzzled me. Now I know why. You are a messenger of God, my love. My mother is a believer in such things and I am sure she will spread the word.' And thus the Saint of Patherson was born to the public at large."

"A year after the betrothal Tonia and Gianni were married. Everybody was so happy and well wishing to the happy couple that gave to the festivities a touch of grandeur; the bride and the groom radiating happiness looked at each other in a dreamy like state. Tonia in her white dress and veil looked like more as an angel then a living person. When they entered the church even though nobody was near the organ it started playing a beautiful melody by itself. The people were stunned for few minutes and although they did not understand what was happening they started clapping their hands chanting "long live the bride and groom!" The episode of the organ was never forgotten and brought substantiation and trust to what followed one year later. It had been a while since people talked about Tonia as being different. But everybody remembered the quasi miracles they had heard about her. It was well known that if anything was wrong when she was around, everything would adjust by itself. If someone was sick, that person would get well. Every night for a while, Tonia would dream about seeing a long line of people standing behind her door waiting. She spoke with her husband and her parents about her dream. All of them agreed that, clearly, it was the will of God that she help people, her gift was not hers to keep secret. It had been given to her to help people. And so, Tonia knew of some friends that were sick. Accompanied by her mother, she went to visit the sick and was able to heal them then and there by laying her hands on them."

"The news of her gift spread immediately all over the town and soon after, the country. The newspapers wrote about it, even by the radio daily news the people were informed of Tonia's gift. The line of people behind her door that she had seen in her dreams became a reality. People in need were coming from all over the country and neighboring countries. The people that consulted her went there for three reasons: for their health, for their children's future, and for their enterprises if they had any going on. Tonia was more a healer then she was a fortune teller. But she tried to answer all their questions and she was never wrong. Many women kneeled in front of her, prayed to her, and she didn't like it. 'you have to pray to God' she would say, 'I am only his servant' There was something a little peculiar about her healing procedures; after laying on hands and the consultation she would tell everybody to wash themselves with salt. Salt in those days was thought to be a powerful disinfectant. As time went by people were getting better and at times completely cured of dangerous infective sicknesses. The line of people in need was always growing to the point that the saint was working from the small hours of the day to the late hours of the night. Sometimes there were emergencies during the night. No one was ever turned away. The Saint was praised and loved by all, only the church was skeptical and non committal. An influential lady of the town went to visit her, more to meet with her and see for herself if what the people said was true, she was impressed by the beauty and gentleness of the Saint. She too asked her for help, her name was Cheli. She was very pretty and on the heavy side. She was concerned about one of her daughters who refused to get married on account of a young man she had met when she was only thirteen years old. The guy was really sick and she had promised to herself that she would not marry anyone but him. Then she asked about the rest of her family. The Saint after listening to the story took Cheli's hands in hers and said, "Cheli, I am very sorry, there is no hope that this young man will ever get well, he will keep your daughter waiting for twenty years before she finally will give up on him, and then it will be hard for her to find someone good, but in the end she will be OK. Cheli as far as your other question is concerned; your heart will be pierced by a sword and your life will change dramatically for the worse but, again, everything will get better in time, but be prepared for what is to come, good lady, as God will never abandon you. Keep your faith in him." Cheli thanked her and with a heavy heart left ending her visit with the Saint. When she went home, Cheli told everything to her husband who dismissed the whole thing saying that the saint was a fake as he shook his head. Then he continued, "Forget about the saint. She does all this to make money. What does she know? She does all this for the money," and left.

After a year or so from that day the town, the district, and the Country stood speechless, incredulous, and heartbroken at the news that their beloved Saint had died during the night. She was found dead by her husband who was inconsolable. People were weeping in the streets, they went to her home, and held a three days wake outside the house. Everybody missed Tonia. She had been a spark of light from heaven for so many and they would never forget her. It was not long before all the predictions of the Saint to Cheli came to pass. Her first son a week after becoming a lawyer, died of meningitis, Cheli and her husband were devastated to the point that they let their thriving business go to pieces and within six months they had lost everything. They had to sell all the assets they had at a loss and move to another region of the Country. People were wondering why Tonia died? Was it because the people had become too dependent on her? Or was it a message from God to tell us, once more, to be prepared because life is not a given, we all must die one day, no matter who we are and what we do, only God is steadfast and the hope of heaven is for all that believe and seek it." Mrs. Figone had ended her story about her daughter. So she invited all of the children to go back from the porch into the living room and have cookies with her. The next day she left.

The Holy Thorn

*O*utside the house of Pontius* Pilate there was a
screaming crowd, some people were screaming and weeping because the authorities condemned an innocent man to crucifixion. Others were
jubilant calling the name of Barabbas who the crowd
graced with life instead of Jesus of Nazareth; many were
cussing against the Romans at large.

The authorities condemned Jesus Christ of Nazareth
to carry the cross to Golgotha where the government
would crucify him. The soldiers scourged Jesus and
crowned him with a crown of thorns before marching
him to his execution. They pushed the thorns into his
cranium and the blood trickled on his forehead and
face.

During his trip to Golgotha, he fell on the ground
three times. When he fell the third time, a thorn from
his crown broke and fell to the street. However, no
one noticed it. A man helped him get up and the cruel

macabre trip continued, to Golgotha where the government crucified the son of God until he died.

Agnes the daughter of the butcher Samuel who was a servant girl of one of the centurions that accompanied Jesus to Golgotha wished with all her heart to accompany Jesus. Agnes was a very pretty girl with black eyes and black hair. She was very thin. She went to the temple because her father was very religious but she didn't like what was going on around her. There was too much greed, too much disrespect for the house of God. People crowded the stairway to the temple selling and buying all kinds of merchandise. The Synagogue looked like more of a supermarket than a place of worship. Agnes dreamed to meet a good man, get married and have children, she loved children. Agnes had not witnessed Jesus' trial but from the inside of the palace where she worked as a maid heard the uproar and screaming of the crowd. At home, she would hear from her father who told her mother how much he liked Jesus and of his anguish for not being able to help him in any way.

Centurion Petronius, Agnes employer, was a roman soldier trained to command and obey orders. He was not a lover of the Jewish people but he believed in justice and was very honest. He did not believe in Jesus' miracles and preaching, but he believed that Jesus was innocent. He believed that he was not a threat to the Roman power in Judea, and he knew that he would help him, if he could. However, he felt he could not help Jesus because he had to protect his family. He was a typical roman soldier. He was tall, thin, and very handsome. He was worried about his family, also, because another child would soon arrive. Petronius' job was not very secure because many other soldiers were coming from Rome to help Herod subjugate the many rebellious Jews that wanted the Romans out of Judea. Petronius, after five years of living and serving in Judea, had not mastered the Jewish language, which made him a liability. He, during the trip to Golgotha never beat or screamed at Jesus.

Agnes wanted to go to follow Jesus to Golgotha; she wanted to see and comfort the just man who would die on a cross, if possible. She was upset because the people chose Jesus instead of Barabbas who was a criminal. She asked her supervisor permission to leave early that day. The supervisor said yes, but only if she did all her chores for the day. Agnes did her best but when she was done the procession that followed Jesus was far away. Agnes started running trying to catch up and see Jesus but the procession was too far ahead to be reached. Agnes started to weep and sat down in the middle of the street. After awhile a little red object caught her eyes, she instinctively reached out with both her hands and picked it up. The little object was wet, she could not make out what it was then she accidentally pricked her middle finger and she realized that it was a thorn, it was a thorn wet with blood, she put it on the palm of her hand, and she looked at it mesmerized. Then it came to her that it was one thorn from Jesus' Crown of thorns. An overpowering emotion took hold of her, and she started weeping again. "Oh Jesus," she prayed, "help me believe that you are the son of God as you say you are.

After praying, Agnes felt warm, and the bleeding face of Jesus appeared to her for an instant. She jumped up and looked around her but she saw no one. She started weeping again but this time she was weeping because she was happy.

Agnes knew that Jesus had heard her. She was happy and in love with the universe. Jesus, she knew, had come to her and that the love of Jesus would be with her always. She decided to keep and hide the thorn for good luck. He was a just man and the son of God. Keeping the thorn would do her no harm. She went home put the thorn in a box then she put it in locket with a chain and put it around her neck. She again felt comforted and warm, she felt light and happier than she had ever felt before. She often thought about Jesus and felt sorry that she never saw him. Months went by, but she never forgot the sad bleeding face of Jesus. Her work was going well the supervisor complemented her often for her dedication and good work. Priscilla, Petronius's wife was pregnant, and she would soon have a baby. Towards the end of the pregnancy of Petronius' wife, Petronius promoted Agnes to be Priscilla's personal maid.

Priscilla was a very beautiful woman. She wore her blond hair long. She had blue eyes and liked to wear expensive ornaments. She was a good mother who, most of the time, cared for her young children personally. She was a good mistress for her staff too. Priscilla indulged herself by buying flowers for the house and herself every day. She liked to dress well and often organized parties for Petronius' friends.

One day Petronius fetched Agnes in the middle of the night because Priscilla had started giving birth and things were not going well. The baby was coming out bottom first instead of headfirst. The midwife and all the other people attending Priscilla knew that only a miracle could save her and the baby. He had fetched Agnes to take care of the two children that he feared would be soon motherless. He loved his wife very much. He was very upset and hardly could control his emotions. After making sure that the children were OK, Agnes went to look for Petronius. She finally heard a strange soft noise, she realized with anguish that it was Petronius hidden by a window drape, he was silently weeping.

She didn't dare go to him or call to him under the circumstances. Men and especially a Centurion were not supposed to weep! Agnes, for a moment, didn't know what to do; she had to find a way to talk to him. She must talk to him. Calling out to him was impossible, it would be a dishonor to be found weeping by a servant. She knew that she could get killed for it; on the other hand, her mistress was dying. So she ran to the kitchen, picked up a large dish, and returned to the room were Petronius was still weeping. She pretended to fall and smashed the dish on the floor. Petronius froze but Agnes started screaming oh God Help me what am I going to do? My master will kill me this was a precious dish. Agnes made sure she didn't look up while she was gathering, slowly, the pieces of the broken dish. This excuse gave Petronius time to compose himself. In fact, Petronius pretending to come from the other room screamed,

"Agnes, what are you doing on the floor are you hurt"? "No master, forgive me master, I fell and broke the dish. I was looking for you. I came to tell you that there is a way to save Lady Priscilla" "How? What can we do? Tell me, Agnes, tell me what to do!" While the ashen face of Petronius was changing with the light and comfort of hope, Agnes told him "Master can you tell the women to let me be alone with the mistress for a moment? You can be with me but everybody else has to go, Master I am sure I have the cure." Since the doctors in attendance told Petronius that there was no hope for Priscilla, and he knew how dependable and truthful Agnes was, so he trusted that Agnes could help Prisicilla. Petronius and Agnes entered the birth room, and they sent everybody out. Agnes hurried to her mistress bed fell on her knees took out from her neck the locket and put it on the neck of the dying Priscilla and started praying to Jesus. She said, "Dear Jesus, save her. Save her!" Almost immediately, Priscilla jerked and sat up in bed touching her belly. She started screaming again, but the screaming baby who had changed position covered her screams. He came out head first of his own accord. Before anyone could come in from the antechamber Agnes left the room. Petronius after ascertaining that his wife was well went to look for Agnes. Agnes had resumed her usual work, but with trepidation was expecting to be called to explain. It didn't take long for Petronius to find Agnes and upon finding her he took both her hands in his and said "Agnes don't be afraid. You saved my family and me with your intervention. I would like to know what the magic in your locket is." "My master" answered the shaking Agnes "it is not magic in my locket. In my locket there is one of the thorns that pierced the head of Jesus of Nazareth. I wanted to follow him and I did try to reach the procession but it was too far away for me to reach it, so I sat in the middle of the street weeping, then I noticed the thorn covered with blood on the ground and picked it up and put it in the locket for good luck. Since then I noticed that everything started going well for me and that I was happy all the time. When I heard that my mistress was going to die I thought of the thorn of Jesus in my locket and I wanted to see if it would bring her luck too." "It did Agnes, it did; my wife is well and my baby boy is well too. I am very grateful to you. What can I do for you? Ask and if I can I will do it for you, you know that while at my service you cannot talk about this to anybody as, it would be dangerous for myself and my family." "Thank you, my master, thank you! I am ashamed to have to take advantage of your offer so soon, but since you offered to help me, I will take advantage of your generosity. I am in love with one of your soldiers, and I believe that he is in love with me too, would you allow for us to get married?" "How about your family, Agnes will they allow you to marry a Roman? Let me think about it Agnes. I will find a way, you are a free woman, I am sure I can help you." A very happy Agnes fell on her knees and profusely thanked Petronius. Petronius, very happy now, informed his superiors and kingship of the happy event and after being congratulated his superior gave him one Month rest to spend with his family. Petronius didn't waste any time. He sent a letter to his brother explaining his debt to Agnes and his wish to help her marry Tiberianus. Tiberianus was a good soldier and a very handsome one; he was in love with Agnes, and he was willing to do anything to marry her. Tiberianus was not very tall, he was of average height, he had black hair and brown eyes he could play the Greek instrument called the "Lyre" and was always happy to play it. In less than a Month Rome, called Tiberianus for duty and Agnes found a placement as a maid in the household of Petronius' brother. Before Tiberianus and Agnes married, they found a house to start their life together in the beautiful city of Ostia where Petronius' brother lived. After they married they moved into the house. Agnes never got back her locket, Priscilla would not separate from it. Agnes did not mind much because she knew that Jesus would be in her heart forever.

In the Tunnel

I became aware of myself looking up under a large tree. I must have fallen asleep. Upon waking up, I found my mind was blank. I could not remember anything. Wait a minute. I remember now. I think that I passed out while looking at an image of my mother. Was it like that? I am confused. Yes, the lovely concerned face of my mother was looking at me when I passed out or I fell asleep. Then I heard a sneeze. I jumped and started to look for shelter to hide. On the other side of the tree, almost behind it, there was a man. He leisurely sat on a large tree root while eating one of the yellow fruits. "Don't be afraid. My name is Petrass and I was expecting you," he said it while both looking at me and offering me a piece of his fruit. I almost grabbed the fruit from his hands and devoured it. Petrass was a tall man who wore a very ornate long white tunic. The tunic ornaments were in gold and showed large multicolored birds nestling on white and yellow branches with leaves and flowers. He seemed still to be young. His hairs were black, his eyes a clear green. He smiled easily and his smile filled me with trust and respect for him. I no longer was afraid of him; actually, I felt safe. He said, "What is your name? Where do you come from? How old are you? I knew you would come but that was all I knew." I replied, "Stasia, my name is Stasia. I come from a small town called Licastris. I came here because I have always been a very curious child. I am eleven years old. If I did not know the how and why of anything that sounded strange or interesting to me, I would investigate it until I understood what happened. Since I was very young I, often enough, would hear that underneath our town, there was a tunnel or a cavern. Countless people through the years went inside this tunnel to see what it was all about, and never came back, so much so, that the mayor of the town had to put iron gates in front of the entrance to avoid people going inside, never to return. On a day that my three older brothers were talking about the tunnel and the mystery that surrounded it, I made my mind up to go to the place to find out if the story of the tunnel was true. My mother also listened because she knew how curious I was. She said that my brothers' speculations were not true and forbade me to go anywhere especially to the cavern or tunnel. I think that it is more appropriate to call it a tunnel because it is long and narrow. I made the decision to go to see the tunnel.

On a Monday morning when most of the people in the town were out working, I went to see the tunnel. I was afraid and remorseful about disobeying my mother. 'I will not go inside.' I told myself, I am going just to see it. I told myself that I will not stay long, I will just look at it, then I will come back home immediately. There was a legend attached to the tunnel and it was that in exchange for safe access three young babies had to die in front of the entrance. Some say that three young babies must die to enter it. I forgot about this legend and upon remembering it, I got scared. I almost turned back home. Then I said to myself, 'This can't be true, it is only a legend. Who would kill three babies?' Besides, the rusted entrance gate would not open and the whole area was in disrepair. There was no one to kill anybody. I also remembered that my brothers had mentioned that there were vipers and scorpions around the entrance too. I sat down on the grass to think. Kill three babies. Impossible, no one could do that. There were many white stones all around me and I began to play with them. Without thinking, I arranged the stones to look like three small dolls. Each doll had a head, two arms, two legs, and a body. At that moment, I heard a crashing noise and a thunder. I jumped while my heart was beating violently and the lovely face of my mother was dancing if front of my eyes. I started to run, but in a matter of seconds, something propelled me into the tunnel. At this point, I lost consciousness. I must have fallen asleep. Upon waking up, I found myself here under a very large tree. The tree was full of strange fruits. They were orange in color and seemed quite ripe. I was hungry. I needed to eat. I was also cold. I looked around to find shelter in which I could warm myself. To my chagrin, I realized that I was in a strange place; then I heard you sneeze."

Petrass looked at me for a few seconds, and then he said, "Yes you are the first one that came here after the world as we knew it disappeared. At that time, I was the high priest and you were my daughter. You were as young as you are now. The Gods required your sacrifice on the altar to pacify them for all the city's sins. You would pacify the gods for our people totally degrading the Gods as well as the other sins of the people of Licastris. You are back now and we must complete the sacrifice ritual to appease the Gods." I said, "It cannot be, Petrass. I am sure that I have never seen this place before. If the city was previously destroyed, then there is no longer any need for a sacrifice to appease the gods anymore." "You don't remember, Stasia. You have been born many times since then. Let me tell you what happened, how the city deteriorated to require the human sacrifices to appease the Gods. You will see by yourself that the people had become slaves of greed, lust, and their degree of cruelty reached beyond anybody's endurance. Stasia, please, sit here by me, and you shall experience everything." Although what Petrass had told me, troubled me, I was not afraid and sat down. I became a little drowsy and looked around. I was in what seemed a large expanse of land. Far away, I could see a hill. On the hill, there was a large temple with colonnades and arcs. On the back of it, there were tall trees and very large bushes. Between the bushes and the trees, there were many rows of small headstones and mausoleums. Some of the mausoleums sent small clouds of white smoke up to the sky. Then I became aware of a soft somber melancholy music and the desperate cries of a woman. Many people seemed to be following a hearse. The woman called with sobs and shrieks the name of her son Camillus. She was saying "Camillus, my dear son, how could your father do this to you? You adorable boy, the love of my heart, what am I going to do? Your heart may live in someone else's body but I cannot see or touch it. I cannot feel it. I will not be able to see your beautiful smile, your playful eyes, and feel your arms around my neck. I used to listen to your stories when you returned from school. You, my love, will never come to me again. I cannot console you when you are in pain or share your joy when you are happy. I will never forget you or forgive your father for selling your body to a rich man. The man wanted your heart. He needed to transplant it into his sick son's body. He did not have the sole right to do this because you are my son too. I promise you that I will go to the consul to report him. I will avenge you. I cannot live without you. I will be happy again only when I will rejoin you.

Saddened by all this crying and weeping, I asked Petrass, who was sitting on a bench close to mine and who was wiping his eyes, what had happened. He looked at me with dreamy red eyes and answered, "These people are taking what is left of Camillus' body to the burning factory of the dead. Camillus was the son of the crying woman. Her husband sold his son's heart to a rich man for a thousand quiros. "But how," said I, "is this possible? How come? Don't you have laws here that protect people from such crimes?" "I see," he answered, "that you act like foreigner!" "Camillus' father is poor; he did not have a job. He found a good price for his son's heart and sold it on the black market. Mr. Fibulas needed a heart for his sick son. So he went to the market and bought poor Camillus' heart. Naturally he had to buy the child first, then he brought him to the hospital and two doctors did the transplant." I was horrified and jumped up while saying, "But what happened is terrible! Camillus was a human being." He looked at me for a long while, then he said, "Sit down, if you please, I see from your attire that you come from another part of the world. Where do you come from?" "Not from far," I answered; "I got lost, fell asleep, and I just woke up here. As matter of fact, I don't know where I am. Please sir, where am I?" He answered, "You are in the grand city of Licastris. As you can see from the view that we enjoy from here, it is a beautiful rich city." I looked around following his hand and could see a very large extension of space, where stood myriad of houses with flowers in window boxes that were whitish in color surrounded by a lot of trees with large leaves. The sky was free of clouds and had an intense blue color. The roads were large, and paved with strange colored stones. It seemed to be cement but I was not sure. Little strange light machines were flying in the air.

A few people were around; men and women dressed in tunic like clothes. All together, the place was very nice. The sounds all around us were those of a big city starting to go through the responsibilities and toils of the day. I looked back at the old man, and smiled. I said,

"You were explaining to me about the funeral, I admired this beautiful view and I forgot. What is your name?" The old man said, "As I told you, my name is Petrass. I am the guardian of the Necropolis yonder. I prepare the pyres of the dead people and attend to the ashes afterwards. I love my job because keeps me in touch with the last reality in this world, and it keeps me prepared to meet the Divinities above,

When I was young," he started, "no one would ever think to do something like that, not to Camillus or anybody else. We nurtured the human body and respected it from birth to death. Now it is a common practice to sell and buy any healthy part of a handicapped person's body, any healthy part of a terminally ill person's body, and any healthy part of abandoned child's body. If within two weeks a set of parents can be found that will care for the abandoned child, and the child is very healthy; then they can live and be cared for in homes at the expense of the government." "Oh! My god," I said. "Is everybody gone mad in this city? This is very dangerous for everybody." "No, not for everybody," answered Petrass, "as I just told you, only for the terminally ill, the handicapped, and the abandoned children. If there were no black market, where you find the body parts at a very high price, then without organ transplants many sick people would die. The black market naturally is against the law. Nevertheless, rich people can buy the organs on the black market with impunity. The body parts bought on the black market are good organs procured from people." "But how is it done?" "The handicapped people are well treated until their organs are needed, then doctors operate on them and they transplant the needed organ into the new body. The organs of the slaves are sold for a very cheap price, when the slaves are no longer useful for work." I replied, "How horrible. How did this barbaric atrocity start?"

Petrass said, "How did it start? Well," he said, "many years ago a doctor, he was a genius you know, and I believe that if he had known that something like the black market would happen, he would not have done it. He wanted to prove to the world that people with heart disease did not have to die young. He successfully removed the heart from a patient near death and transplanted the heart into the heart cavity of a patient that otherwise would have died because his heart did not fully function anymore. It was a big success. It was a grandiose happening. People believed that medical science had touched the apex of knowledge and human endeavor. Many successful operations followed the first and this was just the beginning. After that, many other doctors tried to transplant the heart, some with more success than others. The main problem seemed to be the rejection of the transplanted organ by the body. However, someone found a way of treating the transplant's cells to make the transplanted organ look like the body's original organ. Within a few years, a heart transplant was not so difficult. After the heart, doctors could transplant many other organs, and so the commercialization of human body parts began.

At first, dying people donated the body organs, but

because there were not enough donations, little by little, medical personal and people in need of body organs purchased body organs in the black market. It did not take a long time until people in need of body parts that could not afford to buy the body parts began to riot and kill each other. Some people while they were fighting had accomplices ready to extract the needed organs and run away to sell or use them. The fights lately occurred everywhere. People just disappeared and their skeletons were found later, put in sacks and hurriedly buried or dumped in garbage cans. The law at this point could no longer pretend not to know, and groups of armed police-men scurried around on the streets, especially at night. The police caught people procuring body parts. The law jailed and condemned them to forced labor plus a fine of a thousand quiros. The people that did not have the money to pay the fine had to clean the streets for twice the labor hours instead of the money owed. It was a true abomination and someone had to stop it. For a while, the new law seemed to work. Then slowly the slaughter in the streets began again. They organized themselves so that people would disappear and no one ever saw them again. The body organ trade was very lucrative on the black market. The government knew it. The number of the police officers increased but the trade kept growing until the police found the still bleeding body of a small child without his internal body parts, only the head of the young body was still there.

Again, after a few years, the government passed a law that permitted parents to sell organs from all children with imperfect bodies for organ replacement. Doctors could use all terminally sick people's healthy organs for organ replacement. The ordinance did not stop the black market just the same. However, it seemed that the killings and the disappearances slowed down a bit. The doctors held the women that they thought carried an imperfect fetus in the hospital until they gave birth. After the birth, doctors sent the mothers home and raised the child as a body part donor. The women did not like it and some of them killed themselves before leaving the hospital. It was horrible. The gods complained for a long time by sending earth tremors, floods, and lightning from the sky. One time the sun disappeared from the sky for three days. The gods dumped the world into total darkness. The Augurs warned everybody that the gods were mad and that everyone must respect the right of anyone to live, or the world, as they knew it, would disappear. At this point, the old man stopped talking and looked at me again; he looked at me intently and said, "Don't be distressed! Things are better now. Although there is more order now, the market to sell human organs is against the rules of the land. Nevertheless, it is the law. Now, we bury the dead with dignity. If the police catch someone cheating, the law punishes him with crucifixion. You are still young and you too will get used to this abomination. After so many years, I cannot say that I got used to it. I find it horrific and barbaric.

However, all accept, as I told you that if a young person is terminally sick, deformed, or cannot properly care for themselves; it is legal to use their useful organs as replacement body parts. By the way Stasia, you look tired please have a fruit. It is good and nutritious," so saying Petrass handed to me what looked like a very large apple. I was indeed very hungry and took the fruit. It was delicious. It did not taste like an apple but it looked very much like an apple. Petrass, still looking directly at me, said;"You dress in a very strange fashion." "For what you told me Petrass, I must come from your future. Petrass, I came to find out how the mysterious tunnel underneath our city came to be. I believe that you are telling me why. It seems that a catastrophic earthquake destroyed this beautiful immense city. The gods sent it as a punishment for the atrocities the doctors committed against humanity and decency. Only a few small hills, very deep tunnels and canyons remained. I came from one of the largest hills where people found shelter after the earthquake. "Yes, I was here when it happened and I was expecting you. The oracle of Tibus, predicted the destruction of this infamous, sinful city. No one will ever forget our iniquity for thousands of years until a simple unassuming woman, descending from the house of the goddess Teclas, would come here to make known the horrific sins of this city and free us from the curse of Siscarius.

Please, sit down and I will tell you everything that happened here that so much displeased the gods that they almost destroyed it. Looking as far as the horizon you will see and live the life of those days. Life was lived richly, lasciviously, lewdly, and dissolutely by the people in charge and in command. They lived in palaces surrounded by ornate colonnades and large extensions of multicolored gardens almost covered with large flowers and green foliage. Here and there were deep ponds of water where fishes of all sizes and shapes swam all day long. A line of tall large trees ran down the middle of the estate. It divided the estate symmetrically so that you can see fruit trees and vegetables growing on the right side and a large variety of medicinal bushes of all kinds grew on the left side. To the left of the row of tall trees was a large medicine factory. A long time ago, there was a cure available for any kind of disease. It is divided in departments. For each of the body's afflictions there is a concoction, or medicine to cure everything.

Not far from the medicine factory there is an air Carson factory. Each Carson has the capability to transport two people at the height of 29 to one hundred and thirty feet and at the maximum speed of zero to ten kilometers per hour. These are the machines you see traveling in the air. Electricity propelled the Carson and a light element provided the lift. A mechanism combines oxygen and hydrogen together to create electricity, which controls the motion. While a storage bladder for the light element, hydrogen provides lift for the vehicle. These Carsons are cheap and convenient. Each family must have at least one to ride to work, the city, hospitals, or just for fun. Everybody must have one to go around. With one quiros, anybody can go and come back from the medicine factory. For larger trips, bigger and more expensive Carsons are used. For the longer trips, bigger Carsons used a regulated route. Regulated routes had different speed groups and all the travelers had to use the same speed in that speed group of the route. Carsons had to descend to the lowest speed group to exit the route. Children could not graduate from school if they did not learn to use the Carson. The law did not allow women to ride the big Carson because if they were pregnant, everyone believed that the air motion was bad for the fetus.

Men and women unless incapacitated by sickness or other justifiable problems worked two shifts. The first shift worked from eight in the morning to one in the afternoon. The second shift was from two in the afternoon until seven in the evening. Eunuchs prepared the medication. In fact, no one else could prepare the medication because medicine production for the laborers was dangerous. There was a law against castration, but no one ever enforced the law because the laborers were mostly slaves. The richest people of the town owned the factories, but they wanted more money and more riches. The elders got together to devise a way to make the medicine factory yield more money. There were five elders or chiefs of the factory - Ciros, Carmelius, Jacintus, Camaiculus, and Cesarius. The chief elder was 50 years old. He was a tall cruel man whose big pleasure in life was to inflict the most heinous torments on the slaves that dared to look him in the face. Carmaiculus was a sex maniac who would invite his friends to rape young virgin slaves and young innocent boys after every banquet in his home. He would claim the right to start the orgy. Carmaiculus also liked a lot of food, which he would eat with a voracious appetite. At the age of thirty-five, he needed two attendants to sit down and get up, he, also liked to torture small animals. Cesarius was a different kind of a brute. He was married. He had three daughters that he adored, but to have those daughters married he needed to supply each of them with an expensive trousseau and many slaves. His wife liked to buy all kinds of expensive things and openly cheated on him. These five men after few meetings and long discussions decided to make more money, so they diluted the medicines. They added other particular concoctions that would make people sick with side effects, not cure them. These concoctions were introduced a few at the time and were given mainly to the people at large. After a while, people started getting sick and complaining. Too many people were sick and no one knew why. Siscarius was the high consul of the city. He was a wise just man. He made sure that in any situation nothing got out of hand. He had divided the enormous city into departments. For each department, a legate administered the department's affairs. Once a month the legates met to discuss the life of the city and exchange ideas. Siscarius was against the merchandising of human organs but because people did it for centuries, it was very hard to stop doing it completely. He did not see too much wrong with the euthanasia of the sick and crippled but he did not like it very much either. The last meeting brought to his attention that more people were dying than usual. He began to investigate because there was no good explanation for it. He created a new department with the best capable investigators he knew.

Siscarius was a tall strong man. He was handsome and dressed well. He participated in all the games given in all sectors of the city. He was an honest man and everyone respected him. He was a widower. He had three children one boy and two girls. His wife died of childbirth when his twin daughters were born. Oranus, the boy, was twenty years old. He was very handsome, very tall, slim, and almost athletic. He was very smart. He loved sports and beautiful women. The two Siscarius's daughters were two true beauties. Siscarius named them Riasis and Sarias They were both blond and they had big blue eyes. They were of medium height and weight, they wore curly hair and their tunics were elegant and adorned with flowers. Siscarius adored them. He dreaded the day when they would belong to other men. His life revolved around his family and his city since his wife died.

Siscarius immediately chose the best group of investigators. He had given them special powers and sent them to find the truth. He divided them in three groups. One group would work within the pharmaceutical department; the second group would work with the medical department and the third group in the hospitals. It took a while to ascertain that something was very wrong with the manufacturing of the medications. In fact, an elite group of dishonest pharmacists used the wrong ingredients to manufacture medication for a specific illness so that it would worsen the ailment instead of curing it. Accordingly, many doctors and hospital staff went along with the pharmaceutical company for large sums of money paid under the table.

At times people seemed to get well from one sickness, but after a short time, they would get sicker or require a change in their medication. Most of the sick people were sick for life. They would take one or two medications, but there were patients that took up to ten or more medications. The people in charge of the production of medication in general became very rich. Siscarius was not a man that was satisfied with hearsay information. Before accusing anybody, he required proof. He had to have concrete proof. He under an assumed name pretended to be sick. He went to a doctor of good standing with the populace and complained of stomachache. The doctor listened to him touched him and then gave him some herbal syrup with instructions to take it twice a day and if the pain did not go away to come back to him again. Siscarius went back to his doctor who after analyzing the medication found out that the medication would lessen the symptoms at first, but after awhile the pain would return. Siscarius compared the medication given to him by the doctor with the actual medication for the ailment, they did not agree with one another at all. The first vial contained a small sedative. With the proof in his hands Siscarius, began to think of a way to solve the problem. He opened a new department of medicine production and he recruited a few honest pharmacists, doctors, and hospital workers that he could find. It was not easy but at the end of a year, Siscarius fired the pharmaceutical staff, the doctors, and hospital workers who he now called the silent killers. Now he arrested, tried, and punished the corrupt ones who betrayed the sick. They had two choices of punishment. They could die by crucifixion or by burning at the stake. It took a long time to execute all the guilty parties. It took almost a year. During this time, the relatives of the executed and the enemies of Siscarius armed themselves and declared war on Siscarius and his government. Siscarius fought with all his might but his enemies were strong and well prepared. They denied any wrongdoing and spread lies and money all around the city to make as many allies as they could. In less than a year, Siscarius enemies captured the government's army and the city. Siscarius, with a few loyal soldiers, ran to his home to rescue his daughters. The two young girls were disrobed, laid down on two rough mattresses with their arms and legs stretched out, and a long line of brutes raped them. Siscarius, at the sight of his violated daughters screaming for help, lost his head and with his troops began to slaughter all those that participated. Then he killed his daughters and screamed, "Citizens of this damned perverted and sinful city, I curse you. I curse you for hundreds of generations to come. Your greed and lust has gone beyond the limit of anyone's endurance. Your city, your homes will be destroyed. After you purged yourselves of your sins and sacrileges, you may begin again to rebuild your city. However, you will never have the power and the glory that you had until today. Then he looked at the dead bodies of his children, screamed like a terrified animal, and plunged his dagger into his heart. At the same moment, the sky began to rumble and the earthquake that ended the biggest city of that time began.

The March 8th Earthquake

*A*n expected event occurs every year that the entire town joins in sharing. It is the cornerstone of the town's culture. When it happens, it seems a sad awakening for thousands of people. It starts with the pealing of the church bells that play a melancholy tune for about ten minutes. The hurried opening of windows, balcony doors, and the street doors of the lower flats follow it. A few minutes later candles illuminate all the windows, balcony doors and doors. The people that forgot or did not know why the sudden pealing of the bells ran into the streets asking, "What is it? What is it? Why does the church bells toll?" "We remember the eighth of March when the great earthquake came and destroyed La Grand Petilia where thousands of people died. The earthquake lasted for ten minutes and during that time, many long cracks in the earth opened up swallowing or destroying everything around it for miles. People remembered when the earthquake happened by word of mouth. Every year we stop to remember the event and pray for the people that perished on that day. We transmit the memory to you just as older people transmitted it to us. Thousands of people perished in that great earthquake around the year 579 AD. What was left of a territorial expanse of many square miles of flat land were promontories beside large canyons some of which were very deep. Other small creeks and large rivers changed their route to the sea when the ground opened up." All the people learning the facts stood praying and remembering for ten minutes. After the church bells stopped, groups of people formed throughout the town and the older generations recounted to the new generation what they knew because people retold the story every year on the eighth of March to transmit the memories to the next generation.

To me, the candle lighting and the peal of the bells is an expression of love that has always been very touching. There isn't any historical record of this happening. The survivors transmitted to the future generations the terrible tragedy thru this simple lovely ceremony. People repeated this ceremony each year down thru the centuries. It commemorates the earthquake that destroyed the big city that was La Grand Petelia. The devastation was almost complete. Even after so many years, the people of the town would scream, "I wish that the 8th of March would happen again so that I would be taken away with it," when in despair or very upset.

After the tremors ended and the earth movements

stopped from that horrible, disastrous event, the few survivors began to come out from their hideouts very slowly. The sky during the tremors was dark and the clouds low. After the ground stopped moving, the sky cleared and the survivors began to hope again. In the first few weeks, they survived as well as they could. They were eating new vegetation and any small animals that they could catch. They formed groups of people that seemed familiar to one another. They were afraid of strangers. They did not know one another. Then they saw a few birds flying around and chirping. The poor lost survivors began to hope and look at themselves. They did not recognize where they were. They looked at one another with suspicion and distrust. The survivors started to search for people they could trust. Slowly they began to talk and were very happy to understand what they said. They knew that they were speaking the same language. They began to ask questions. While they asked each other what had happened, they became closer and started to understand that the same thing happened to all of them. Additionally, they were able to make sense of what had happened. People began to trust each other. Some of the survivors knew how to ignite fire. Soon everyone built their own fires. Although they knew about earthquakes and tremors of the land, they had never experienced one. The earthquake happened at the start of spring. Now it was summer time, but they knew that the winter would soon come and they had to be prepared. They used caves for shelters just after the earthquake. Now they were in groups, so the groups made plans to rebuild the lives of their members. Once the first group of people formed, other groups quickly formed. They ate what they could find, but what was plentiful to eat and survived the earthquake were the small animals and plants. This provided the food for everybody. There was abundance of broken up wood and iron cast pieces that they used as tools, pots, and utensils.

Eventually, they experienced a very cold winter. They began to establish, small communities, small villages where they could survive. The earthquake had created mountains, large and small promontories, and many deep and large canyons. In all the canyons, there was water in abundance. The problem was transporting the water especially from the deepest canyons. However hard it was, they managed to get enough water to satisfy their needs. They managed to sew together large leaves to make clothes using long thin stems of flax for thread. To stop the water from escaping thru the seams they applied mud over them. In the same way, they made small and large containers for other uses, they gathered wood to make utensils, and they built the first rudimentary small dwellings. They managed to survive and get used to their new way of life. On one of the largest and biggest promontories created by the earthquake, three villages emerged. The village of Licastris originated first. Then another group began to emerge. The second group called their village Camellier and a third hamlet called Pagliore emerged. Each village was about five to six miles from each other. The people of these three communities spoke the same language. It seemed that the inhabitants of each village did not like to mingle with the people of the other two very much. Although they spoke the same language, each village had their own slang and their own life styles that were different from one another. There could have been grudges carried over from before the earthquake, or that they had diverse professions and behaviors that compelled them to be by themselves before the earthquake. The people of Licastris seemed to have been more organized and open to discussion, planning, and sharing. They choose a chief who answered their questions and they respected. He anticipated what to do and organized them to do it. The people of the other two villages kept to themselves, they liked to gather and domesticate animals big and small. They seemed to have been farmers and cattle ranchers. Although they had a rural background, they all wanted to specialize in what they had done before. They did not want to stay together. There was no one in charge in either of the two smaller groups. The people in the smaller centers lived anyway they wanted. This went on for a long time. After a while, everyone obeyed a rough set of unwritten rules. After many millennia of use, the rules slowly grew into laws and regulations. I remember that when I was child, even, after thousands of years, I could notice that they were not too friendly towards each other. Licastris was the first and the biggest of the villages on the promontory. They were more open minded, industrious and in a way more civilized. However as the time went by, the inhabitants lived in some comfort.

Now, Licastris grew into a city after so many

centuries. The people elected Mr. Filottete as the founder of the city. They made a statue of him and placed it in the biggest plaza in the city. The people are industrious, ambitious, and strive to better themselves and the town. The inhabitants built many large elegant houses. The people called biggest houses palaces because the buildings are elegant and have multiple stories. Some were large and comfortable. There, also, are magnificent houses that speak of wealth. There are large commercial buildings with many rooms. Rich people owned these houses. Most of the streets, though narrow, are paved with cobblestones. The most central Streets and the piazzas are paved with cement.

Then a poor friar from the city of Paola built the first church. When people come back home from another city, the spacious beautiful view of St. Francis of Paola's Church always seems enchanting. The church stood on top of the beginning of the promontory, were Licastris stood, very close to the edge. The church is nothing spectacular; it is a white large long Church with a steeple, which contains a full set of bells. The birds fly around it all day long. The bell chamber is open so that the people near the church could hear and wake up with the music of the bells. The people in the church also could hear the chirping and singing of the birds that flew into and around the bell chamber before the bell music started. So did the people near the church. What is almost magic is the feeling one gets when you turn the curve and come up the rise into the town. The first thing you see is the church and a feeling of peace and contentment overcomes you. The church seems to welcome you, to invite you to stop for a moment, and to enjoy the quiet and peace of the place. The view of the valley below is enchanting. The valley is a green large expanse of land. Here and there small houses inhabited by rural people with large cultivated vegetable and animal farms. Beautiful fruit trees of many kinds enrich the scene.

There is a true beautiful story attached to the building of the church. On top of the promontory where now St Francis of Paola church stands the land was bare and dry. Large bushes with thorns and yellow flowers covered it. Masons cut large boulders into parts of the church building. The city of Paola was a small community in the Italian region of Calabria where the monastery of Paola operated helping and teaching the poor. St. Francesco (Francis) was a monk of this community of friars who believed in the power of prayer, charity, and love. He decided to leave the monastery with the blessing of his prior. St. Francesco was born into a rich family and his parents expected him to work in his father's estates. Francesco did not want to hear of it. He loved Jesus and he wanted to care for the children and the poor. Against his parents' wishes, he joined the priesthood. He became a monk and left his convent to accomplish his self-chosen mission to help the poor. His habit was black and belted with a knotted cord; he always wore a hood, and carried a long black stick. He left his monastery, to convert and help all the people that needed his help. He was very poor. He ate when he could and was poorly dressed. When he left the convent, he asked God to let him know with a sign when and where to stop and begin his mission. After Months of walking, praying, helping people during his wanderings he entered Licastris. He was homeless. He slept on the side of the road and helped the farmers in their fields to earn his bread and water. He arrived at the bottom of the hill where the town of Licastris stood. He was very tired his feet were bleeding but he found the strength to walk to the top of the hill into Licastris where he collapsed. When St. Francis woke up, he smelled a delightful perfume. He looked around and found his stick. On the top of the stick to his amazement, he saw a bunch of beautiful white lilies that had grown on top of his stick. He was delighted because he knew that this was god's sign. He knew that God wanted him to start his mission in this place. He immediately felt invigorated so he started looking around to see how he could begin. He envisioned a church and decided to build one. He started to clean the place and began to look for wood. He went looking for tree branches, stones, and anything that was usable to build the church. He actually started the church by putting up a crude cross, which would be his mission. He went around the town to meet and talk with the people. He offered his help in any way he could He began to teach the city's children in the morning. He worked in the fields, he helped the sick, and he ministered to the city's families. He never asked for anything in return. When people asked him if they could give something else to him for his aid, he would answer, "Give me some wood to build my church's meeting hall." He helped the Licastris people so much that, after a while, they got together and built the church for him. The church was long and large with a few niches for holy statues. The steeple stood high on rear of the roof and every day Saint Francis played the bells to wake up the people and invite everyone to pray with him. After he died, the people made him the protector or patron of the town. St. Francis cured the sick. He made all kinds of miracles touching the people that prayed for his help with the first three fingers of his right hand (it was said that the three fingers represented the Father, the Son and the Holy Spirit). In fact, his statue has the flowered stick and the three fingers of his right hand open.

Every year on the anniversary of the completion of the church (on the day that the people first blessed the church), the people celebrate Saint Francis with a feast. They put a statue of him on a large golden pedestal that looks like a cloud. On the cloudlike pedestal are twelve seats where twelve young children sit. They all dressed as a small version of Saint Francis. The children wear a black, long tunic with 'CHARITAS' (CHARITY) embroidered on the breast and the hood in white. A white cord holds the children's tunic together, just as it held Francis' tunic together. Twelve men bid to have the honor of carrying the statue on the cloudlike pedestal with the children. The people of Licastris revered Saint Francis. They carry his statue with the children to all the houses in the town. When they reached a house where someone was sick, they stopped and prayed for the sick in the house.

On the day of the procession, the inhabitants drape all the windows and balconies of the city with silken-damasked tapestries. The procession starts from the church and continues through the largest avenue of the town accompanied by the local musical band to visit every street in the city. A long line of young girls and boys, chanting songs in honor of the saint follow the procession. The children on the cloud look so beautiful they touch your soul, although the children very often cry and want to step down if their parents are not close to them. The parents and the older siblings of the children accompany the procession to care for them. They talk to them and feed them sweets to keep them from crying. The procession finally ends after it reaches the end of the itinerary and proceeds back to the church where all assemble for services.

However, the procession is not all that happens to celebrate the feast of Saint Francis. People make generous offerings for the poor. The people attach or pin to the saint's habit and on the children's hoods the donations, mostly in paper money. After the procession and services end, an impressive show of artificial fireworks illuminates the sky of the town. This lovely procession to celebrate St Francis not only occurs on the feast of St. Francis, but it occurs whenever a crisis happens. The people repeat the procession in any crisis with much fervor. People say that St. Francis has always come through with a miracle when the procession went through the town and the people prayed in the procession. My town, I have to say, is a very devoutly catholic town. We, also, celebrate in the same way the feast of St. Anthony of Padua and the Madonna of the Rosary.

The procession ends at the church of St. Francis, which sits on top of the promontory that was created after the earthquake destroyed the town on the eighth of March millennia ago. After the building of the church it was discovered that under the promontory where the church stands are large caverns, which are long and large. The entrance to the caverns is not far from the church. It is just below the church at the bottom of the promontory. The residents say that the people who survived the great earthquake used these caverns for shelter after the quake had claimed the city. Nevertheless, no one really knows for sure.

Boxing Is a Bloody Dangerous Game

*A**lbera is a little town* nestled at the foot of the mount Arcadia. The mountain is large and tall. It was populated with large, tall ancient trees. On the mountain the trees were so close together that the light hardly filtered through the thick foliage. Some Small houses had a garden, but some of the houses had a chicken coop and a tract of cultivated vegetables. The bigger houses had a barn to keep one or two cows to provide fresh milk daily, as well as the land to grow fodder and vegetables. Some of the houses were embellished with ornate gables and hanging flowers pots. The dark brown doors were strong. The houses were not pretentious but overall the houses looked newish and nice. The neighborhood lots were divided from each other on all sides by a cross hatching of roads. On the right border of the neighborhood was the city hall, while the post office stood on the opposite border. All-around there were a dozen or so of the houses enriched by a two car garage with almost the same style of door. The only difference was in the door color. The houses were all colored green with white windows. At circa half a mile from the center of the small town there was a large and long mall that contained all kinds of shops restaurants, a cinema and a theater. The people seemed to be happy; everybody knew everybody. They were all very friendly with each other.

At 327 Lakeshore lived a family of four people May and Gerald Rubio with their two children Natalie and Gregory. Natalie grew up to be a beautiful girl. She liked music. Her dream was to be an opera singer. She spent all of her time studying and working. She went to the opera house where she worked as an usher. Every time there was a concert. She saved the money to help her mother pay for the household expenses and her music lessons. Since she was very young she had music lessons. She was very good at her music. She dreamed about becoming a famous opera singer.

From the outside it seemed that everyone in this pretty gabled house with so many beautiful flowers lived a happy life. Actually, both the husband and his wife were fighting continuously. They yelled and cussed at each other. Gerald was an invalid. He had been one for almost ten years. When he was young his great dream was to become rich and famous by becoming a champion boxer. He did become a champion and he did become rich. He was so rich that that he could afford to have his own chauffeur. He and his family traveled with his jet. He bought his wife jewels, elegant clothes, and took her to famous theaters. He sent the children to a private school. If the children found themselves behind in their schoolwork he would hire for them private tutors. He was happy to spend lots of money. He had become so famous that it was an honor to fight him.

On the Christmas week of 2001 he was scheduled to fight a match with the European champion. Gerald felt ready and he was sure he would win He was so sure of his victory that he didn't exercise before the match. His wife had a bad feeling. On the night before the match she dreamed that he had fallen in a lake and he had drowned. She begged him not to go or at least postpone the match. Gerald was too sure of himself. He not only did not listen to her, he got mad at her. The first two rounds went in favor of Gerald, but in the third round the opponent got the better of Gerald. He punched Gerald in the head with a terrible blow. Gerald fell in the ring, but while Gerald was falling, his opponent punched him savagely in the forehead, both Gerald's eye began to bleed; the pain must have been atrocious because he passed out. After the referee ended his count and decided the winner. The match ended, but Gerald's eyes continued to bleed profusely.

Gerald was brought to the hospital. It took a very long time for him to recover from his wounds. His eyes had been completely smashed. In the end, he was left with two blind eyes in his face, there was no hope. His vision was completed gone, He was desperate. He went to the best doctors to be cured, He and his wife traveled to all the nations of the civilized world to see eye specialists and hospitals, but no one could restore his sight. He had to resign himself to a life without light. He had spent his money trying to find a cure, so he and his family now found that they were poor. All the riches he had bought had gone into medical expenses and world travel. Gerald's mother and father lived in Albera and Gerald and May had to move into Albera with Gerald's parents. Life was very hard because Gerald was desperate. He needed to occupy his time doing something that he did not need his sight to do. Gerald's doctors advised to find for him something to do, doing nothing all day was driving him crazy. It was necessary for him to do something to pass his time. A job would be ideal but what could he do? Many venues were explored then all in the family agreed that it should be a manual job, it had to be something he could do with his hands.

When he was a child he liked to make Christmas ornaments. He had lost his will to live but his mother that was continually at his side cajoling and talking with him. He slowly began to work at making dolls. At first it was very difficult and very hard, but then he began to remember. He remembered from the past all the little things that he repeatedly performed well. As time went by he started make things and create better things. He never forgot his past glories and riches but he began to live and mix with his family and friends. He didn't talk much about what had happened. It was always in his mind, but he in his mind began to recapture his past and forget the passion he had for his dangerous sport, although his young son seemed to like the sport that ruined his life. He didn't dare talk about it with anybody. Because his wife was adamant about her son not training to fight, she wouldn't allow anybody to even talk about it.

Gregory's son was now a young man reading in old newspapers about the glories of his father. He dreamed to be as good as him and as famous as him when he grew up., After searching his soul long and painfully, he approached his mother on his eighteenth birthday asking if he could follow his father footsteps. May, his mother, looked at him for a long time. She couldn't believe what she was hearing. She was dismayed. Then she jumped up from behind her desk and screamed, "No! Never! Never again! I would rather see you dead before I would see you butchered by a two legged blood thirsty animal in a ring. Your own father didn't fall down. Didn't the fight teach you anything? This is not a sport! This is the animal instinct in man for blood and cruelty. I love you son. There is nothing I would not do for you to make you happy. Will you, please, come with me to the library? I would like to read with you the story of Rome and the gladiators. Please forgive me for upsetting you. I assure you that the word boxing has the power to evoke in me memories of nightmares about denying human progress.

When I studied Roman history in my junior year in high school, I was astounded by the activities in the Roman arenas. The gladiators fought one another to the death in front of a blood thirsty crowd. For the crowd, it became a show of savagery that conjured up my night-mares. I would wake up horrified by the image of the crowd screaming, pleading for the emperor to turn his thumb down in the hope of seeing the blood of innocent people spilled. But the spilling of a man's blood would only drive the crowd to wish for more blood, to want more blood, to demand more blood. So the circle would commence again with the active need for seeing men killed. Examining these nightmares after I woke up, I was impressed by how little the concept of humanity prevailed in those times. At your father's last fight I saw those terrors personally. I have never recovered, but there is a good chance that it will happen to you if you fight. You do not have the speed! There is always someone younger and faster. I would die if my son was disabled. In Roman times the gladiators were slaves who did not have any family to be devastated, while Boxers today have families.

We say "Thank You God. Things have now changed. No more oversized arenas where many fight together." "We now recognize and respect the individual. Now we focus on one man against another man. Man is superior to animals; his genius has brought forth things that seem like sorceries and magic to the men of Roman times. No one could have foreseen such things as TV, to mention just one, back then. When, even now, I accidentally turn on the TV and see a boxing match; I always think of the Roman arenas. What is the difference between a gladiator and a boxer? What is the difference between a roman arena and a boxing arena? It is a set of rules? The gladiators had rules also. Except for matches to death or unconsciousness, there was little difference between their game and boxing. Explaining the bloody game is, maybe, the job of the TV commentators. They lead the cheers and explain the bloody details with instant replays and close-ups, giving their viewers satisfaction and blood. Comparing Boxing to the gladiator matches of the far past shows that now the commentators can concentrate on what is important in today's sport. The commentators excitedly report the most violent punches and do not report punches that score points. They show that very little has changed from the gladiatorial matches of long ago. Certainly the crowds are the same. They hoped, wished, yearned to see someone unconscious, maimed, or killed. The difference between them and the Roman crowd is that today's crowd only cheers the winner while the loser is still on the floor. The gladiatorial crowd also cheered the killing of the loser. No one tracks what has happened to the old fighters. If they did they would see time reveals the toll that the punches take as age accumulates the injuries into disabilities. Look at Muhammad Ali. He now walks around with severe Parkinson's disease and he was essentially undefeated."

Gregory looked a little shaken but not convinced. He tried to talk but May lifted her hand to stop him. She continued, "As incredible as it may seem, parents are not even cautioned by the authorities to keep the children from watching this savage cruel game. What does this game teach them? It teaches them that in a proper setting, and a recognized set of rules it is OK to fight, hit, maim and even kill a human being. Incredibly, the winning boxers become heroes to the crowd and the children. If I were to really define the difference between the two games, it would be that the gladiators were forced to fight. Professional boxers are paid to fight and kill." May looked her son in the eyes said to her son, "Please, Gregory, think about what I told you. If you don't believe me, read this book on Rome's history and customs. It describes the decline of the Roman Empire." Gregory was silent and pensive for a while then he said "Mother I have listened to you and I don't know if I can easily renounce my dream to follow the footsteps of my father. I cannot do what you ask me to do. I have been nursing this dream since I was a young child. I didn't mention it to you earlier because I didn't want to upset you." Because May was trying to talk he stopped her by saying, "Listen mother I will not, as I thought I would before our discussion, do anything to study, learn, or train to enter the fighting ring. I will wait until I have reached full maturity and completed my schooling. I understand your predicament and I promise to you that I will go to school and graduate with honors. I have listened to you and I don't need to read the book because I believe you. I have seen movies with gladiators and their predicament and I either didn't pay attention or I thought that it was a tale. Daddy didn't ever talk about the loss of his eyes. I asked him a few times about it. He always told me time after time that it was an accident and it was too painful for him to talk about. Forgive me mother, but this is the best I can do at this time." May now saw how hard it had been for his son. She hugged him and said, "Thank you my loving and good son. I trust you and I accept your decision. God will help us." Gregory graduated with honors. For his love of his mother and father he gave up his dream of becoming a famous boxer. He never mentioned the subject again and neither did his father dream of his son becoming a champion boxer.

The Assassination of
Carla Sheldon

*C*oming home from the funeral service of her
aunt, Carla Sheldon, Natalie Scott was very sad.
She loved her aunt very much. She had raised her
the best way she knew how. Carla, Natalie's aunt, at the
time of her death was very rich. However, in her youth
she was very poor, very beautiful, incredibly cunning,
and cruel. Because she stopped at nothing to get her
way, she became very rich and powerful. Nevertheless,
her mother always warned her that she should be less
cruel, shed her reputation for being dishonest and ruth-
less because it would not bring her any luck. In the end,
she would have to atone for her wrongdoing because as
the saying goes what goes around comes around. When
she heard that saying, Carla would smile her wicked
smile and get out of the house without giving a thought
to her mother's advice. Mrs. Sheldon, when Carla was at
the worst behavior, would say to her stressed husband,

"Don't worry Paul. She will grow out of it in time. She must be the reincarnation of a bad soul. We love her and we will pray for her." Carla managed, with her usual ingenious and cunning attitude, to build an empire of deceit and cruelty that no woman had ever done before. She was the first daughter of Paul and Mary Sheldon. Paul was a religious man who went to church regularly, helped the poor, and he never denied anybody assistance. He could not understand how Carla could be his daughter or his wife Mary's child. They took comfort with their second daughter, Marguerite, who was a beautiful, good, and loving daughter. On Carla's birthday, they each got a ticket to a concert that would change their lives forever.

Emile was a handsome man of medium height and weight; he had green eyes and reddish hair. He liked to be sociable and he would go to parties and social functions whenever he could make the function. He was a professor of mathematics and sciences. He was very smart and many people considered him a genius. He loved music and masterfully played the violin. At the Fourth of July celebration, that year, he was the main attraction. People came from all over the state to hear him play. He enjoyed playing classical music and he enjoyed being with the people who appreciated his music. During an intermezzo, Emile went to a large refreshment stand on the site of the theater for refreshments and two beautiful women attracted his attention. He, without thinking, headed towards them and with a smile, Emile asked, "can I join you?" Simultaneously, the two ladies answered, "Yes, please do." Carla Sheldon said while extending her hand, "I am Carla Sheldon and this is my sister Marguerite." Emile said, "Nice meeting you." The two sisters said at the same time. "Same here," Emile answered. "My name is Emile Scott. Thank you, I do not think that I can find a plate to eat. The place is packed. Are you new here? I don't think that I saw you before." Marguerite said, "Yes we are new here." Carla kicked Marguerite in the shins, while she looked directly at her crossly as if she wanted her to shut up! It started the beginning of a war between the two sisters who both fell in love with Emile. Emile liked both girls but fell in love with Marguerite. Carla was tall thin with big brown eyes. She had a mane of black curly hair that she wore long and everyone could see that she wore the long hair with pride. She had full lips and a radiant smile. Marguerite was petite, had blue eyes, and blond hair. She had a little French nose, which highlighted her beautiful smile. She laughed often, her laughter sounded like a cascade of pearls and Emile loved it. It was love at first sight for the three of them.

Carla decided that she would marry Emile, no matter what she had to do. He was the valiant prince about whom she had always dreamed. She saw how he was attracted to Marguerite. At that moment, she began to fight for him. She flirted with Emile and asked him to dance with her. She used all the tricks she knew to seduce him but without avail. Emile was nice to her but his eyes were searching for Marguerite. In fact, Emile invited Marguerite to dance as soon as the dance with

Carla ended. While they were twirling around to the sound of a waltz, Carla decided to change her ways to seduce Emile. She began to belittle Marguerite as much as she could. She invited Emile to a musical show in a well-known theatre and did not let Marguerite put a word into the discussion that followed. Carla took hold of Emile completely. Emile accepted the invitation to the theatre. Carla impressed him by her knowledge on the world of music. Nevertheless, he was embarrassed by the way Carla excluded Marguerite from the conversation. Emile did not like Carla but it seemed that she had a hold on him. Carla never stopped talking. She went from one subject to another without interruption. Emile did not have any opportunity to cut into the discussion. Carla went as far as to ask Emile to accompany her to a very important appointment from which she was late. Emile shook hands with Marguerite and hurriedly left with Carla. Carla took Emile to another party were she introduced him to high personalities of the music world. Emile against his will and best judgment enjoyed the party, but, above all, the people he met impressed him. At the end of the party, Emile took Carla home. However, when Carla invited him to go upstairs to her rooms, Emile categorically refused. Something like that had never happened to Carla, she could not believe it. She got very mad and slapped Emile violently in the face. She screamed at him that without her help, he would never go anywhere! In addition, he should not get any ideas about her sister because she was a confused camp follower who would bring to him bad luck. Marguerite was subordinate to her sister completely. They lived in the same apartment building but lived in separate rooms. Carla, after leaving Emile, went directly to Marguerite's place where she beat her savagely and forbade her to see Emile again. Carla worked and was CEO to a large corporation that specialized in the import and export of precious metals. She, with inside information, speculated on the money market winning millions of dollars. She stopped at nothing; she trampled and destroyed many families and at the age of thirty-eight, she was a millionaire. The only thing that she wanted to have and could not was the love of Emile.

After the ill-fated first meeting, Emile stayed away from the Sheldon sisters for a month or so, he knew that he had wounded Carla but he also knew he had fallen in love with Marguerite. As hard as he tried, he could not stop thinking about her, or put her out of his mind. One day when he missed her more than the usual, he went to the school where she taught art to special children. It was not hard for Emile to find Marguerite because the phone book listed her phone number. He called and asked if they could meet. Emile said, "I did not have a chance to get to know you when we first met and I would like very much to talk to you. I like you. And I cannot get you out of my mind!" After a few minutes of silence Marguerite answered, "Oh! Emile, I have thought of you often enough, but I don't think that it is a good idea because my sister forbade me from ever seeing you!" "Marguerite, why don't we have a cup of coffee? We both need to know if we truly like each other, we need to talk to find out our feelings because, now, I think I love you. This could be why your sister did not let us exchange a word. Once we meet again and talk we will know." Marguerite replied, "I am not very sure about it, but I think that there is no harm in meeting just once." Emile said, "Tomorrow is Saturday. Would you like to go into the country to Lake Summit? I was told that one can even fish there and I have a pair of fishing gear." Marguerite answered in a very happy voice, "Yes, yes; I would love to go. Nevertheless, we better go by separate ways to avoid any problem with my sister." They did. After they arrived and saw each other, Marguerite and Emile knew that they were in love. They rushed into each other's arms and spent a glorious day together. They knew that they could not live apart. Marguerite was terrified of Carla and begged Emile to be very careful about Carla. Because Marguerite feared Carla's anger and vehement vengeful ways, she wanted to avoid any of Carla's actions. She suggested that they could find another country, where Emile could find better work, to live and be happy. Within six months, they moved to Italy where they both found jobs. Then they eloped and moved there. After three years, they received a wonderful letter from Carla who amicably scolded them for having married without telling her. She was feeling lonely and she wanted them back in her life. She, too, was married now. She was praying to find them back home when she returned from her honeymoon. Emile and Marguerite were very much in love. A year after their eloping and subsequent marriage they had a baby girl that they adored. Her name was Natalie. She was blond with blue eyes and beautiful like an angel. The first year everything went well. His employers knew Emile was a talented musician. He was always busy and in demand but then things slowly changed. Emile lost a couple of jobs. He was still in demand, but because of the stressed economic situation in Italy, he could not get work. Soon after the war, things had changed and he was not working as much as before. There were times when the concerts that employed Emile closed. They had trouble living when Emile was without work.

At the time of Carla's letter, they were thinking of returning home, not because they were poor, but because they were homesick. They thought that Emil would have better luck as a musician in America. While the two lovers were still thinking to improve their situation, the end of their dreams came crashing down. The most celebrated orchestra, in which Emile played, appeared during a public political function. During the middle of the function when the orchestra was having the intermezzo, Emile, Marguerite, and Natalie sat at a table having refreshments. Three shots rang out! Marguerite saw the shooter and dropped Natalie to the floor. Marguerite and Emile died immediately leaving Natalie on the floor. For a moment, the baby stopped as if she had recognized someone; then she started screaming again on the floor. The police arrived, dispersed the crowd and took the still screaming baby and the dead people to the hospital.

Carla was not expecting to find the baby at the

concert and was appalled to find her with her parents eating and playing with them during the intermezzo. Three-year-old babies don't go to concerts. On the other hand what you expect with parents like hers. She rushed out of the music hall, went to the kitchen below the building, dumped the dishes in the large dishwasher, and left the kitchen in a hurry. She cautiously went to the bathroom. Once in her stall, she changed into the clothes of deliveryman and left the building carrying a large empty box. During her exit, she did not meet anybody. Once out of the building, she took a taxi and went to the airport to catch an intercontinental airplane back to America. Carla never forgave Emil for not wanting her.

Since the fateful concert where she met Emil, she had hated her sister with passion. She wanted her to disappear and never reappear. When she discovered that they had a child and that they were very happy, she wanted their destruction. She thought and imagined many ways to destroy them. She wanted them dead, so they must die. In the beginning, she thought to hire a paid assassin, but she was too smart for that traceable action. It was too dangerous because not only could the assassin blackmail her afterwards, but also they lived in another country, which could create untold problems and dangers. She must find a safe way. How could she do it? She stopped for a moment and then she thought that she could do it herself. After a long pause, she thought why not. If I manage to do it, I will be safe, I am a good planner, and I have the time and the funds to do it.

Above all, I hate them enough to kill them. Yes, yes - tomorrow I will start reading about of how to commit a murder. She was happier now. She got her car and went to the library. She found that she liked thinking about killing them. She found that the anticipation and planning of the murders was like solving a puzzle. It pleased her greatly to anticipate all the ways the police could catch someone and avoid them. Then when she shot them, the pleasure and satisfaction she felt was enormous. She said to herself, "I could get used to this; I get so much pleasure out of it."

In the last five years Carla had got married to a very rich man thirty-five years her senior. Mr. Blount was an investor. He traded in real estate. He began when he was still young. He bought old properties, renovated them, and sold them for a big profit. Three years back his secretary of twenty years was married and moved away with her husband. When Mr. Blount advertised for another secretary, Carla was amongst the many that answered his advertisement. Carla investigated her prospective employers very thoroughly. Her probable employers had to have the qualifications of being single, old enough to be her father and rich. Carla in less than a year was married to Mr. Blount.

After a few years, she decided to get rid of her husband and she choked him with a pillow while sleeping. She did it slowly and mercilessly. She would bring her husband near death and then revive him again. Then she repeated the same thing again. Mr. Blount never woke up completely. He could not scream or defend himself.

After the fourth time that she choked him, Mr. Blount was dead. The doctors said it was a heart attack. This was the only way she saw to become rich. With the insurance and the real estate assets, she became a very rich widow.

After two years, she decided to find another job because she didn't think she was rich enough to stop making money yet. Her victim this time was not an entrepreneur but he had a million dollar life insurance policy. His name was Albert Barton. Albert Barton was nineteen years old when he married his high school sweet heart. He was a handsome young man with a lot of dreams and aspirations. He wanted to become an electronic engineer. He liked to build electronic equipment. He had a creative mind and liked to work with his hands. He often surprised his mother by making little, useful things to make her life easier. He was an A student who planned to achieve great things in his life. However, he met and fell in love with Anne Carter at a wedding party. Anne was a beauty. She was a tall blond who had big blue eyes and a big smile. Her dream was to become a model and she dressed and looked like one. Against her will and best judgment, she fell in love with Albert. They tried to slow their passions for each other because they knew that they had to complete their studies before rushing things. However, they did not make it. Within three months, Anne was pregnant. The two love birds debated about having an abortion. In the end, they decided to keep the baby. After the birth of the baby, Anne would stay home while Albert would find a job and support the family.

Albert found a job easily enough in the financial department of a company that produced precious gems and expensive jewelers. After six months, the management promoted him to manager in the production department because he impressed his supervisor with his knowledge of electronics and his creative ideas just about everything. He made good money and was very happy for that. After the birth of a baby girl, he wanted to provide for his family just in case something happened to him. He bought a large insurance policy to provide for the family if he died. Albert was in very good terms with his manager who was a woman by the name of Carla Sheldon. She liked Albert immediately and began to seduce him. She liked Albert very much and it was a close friendship for a while. Nevertheless, after Albert told her that he had insured his family for a million dollars, Carla decided that she wanted all that money. In short, she wanted to marry Albert to get to the money. She did not make the same mistake as with Emil. She started low. She talked to him often with understanding and trust. She listened to him. She talked to him about all her little problems true or just thought up to get close to him. After a couple of months of this sisterly behavior they began to go to lunch together just to talk about business. In fact, they charged most of their lunches as a business expense.

Since Anne cared for the baby, she was too busy to pay much attention to what Albert did. After a year,

Carla was his lover. He still loved Anne but Carla had become a part of him. He depended upon her for everything that he did. When Anne realized what happened, it was too late. Carla was pressing him to get married because she loved him so much, and people were talking about them. Albert was against the divorce, but Carla was relentless and he acquiesced in the end. After the divorce, the first thing that Carla made him do was to change the insurance beneficiary to her name and the child's name. Finally, they married.

Anne was devastated. She still loved Albert, and it was very hard on her. Anne was a proud woman and she despised Albert for what he had done to her. She decided that with the alimony she could take care of the baby and go to school. Once a week Sally, Albert's and Anne's baby girl spent a Sunday with her father. One Sunday in August, Albert went to get his little girl. He usually went with Carla. This time she told him that she had a business meeting, so she had Anne accompany Albert and Sally. However, she would join them later at the zoo. While on the way to the zoo, a large VW van suddenly sideswiped the car while Albert drove and sang with Anne and his little girl. He lost control of his car, rolled over, and had a fatal accident with the VW. Albert and the baby died instantaneously while the driver ran away. The accident occurred at an intersection that was almost devoid of traffic. No one saw the hit and run driver. A Good Samaritan stopped at the site of the accident to help, but father and child were both dead. George Furley, the Good Samaritan, called the police, but he could not give information on the hit and run driver. He had seen from far away a large van but could not identify the maker of the van or give any other information. After the accident when Anne woke up, she could not remember anything about the accident. The doctors thought that the amnesia was a permanent result of her head trauma during the rollover accident.

The police went to Carla's company to tell her as next of kin of Anne about the accident. They asked her where she was at the time of the accident. She told them she was having an important end of the fiscal year meeting and could prove that she had never left the building from the beginning to the end of the meeting. On the previous night, Carla had changed the time on all the clocks of the company and the established time to meet on the paperwork.

Anne was devastated. She could not believe what had happened! She went into hysterics and stayed in the hospital for quite some time after the accident. It took long time for Anne to recover. Albert without Carla's knowledge had put an a codicil in the will saying that if anything happened to him Anne was to have access to the money to care for herself and their daughter Sally. Carla had not checked the verbiage of Albert's will when she had him change it and when all the legal jargon had been taken care of she had to settle for three quarters of the estate because one quarter of the estate was to take care of Anne and her child. Carla's attorney advised his furious client not to dispute the unclear will of her ex husband. Carla acquiesced because there were insinuations about her love for her ex-husband.

Carla as soon as she could invest the three quarters of a million dollars for maximum profitability. She hired the best people that she could find to run the business. She made successful investments and she was a very rich widow after a few years. She had only one problem, she was unhappy. She against her will and best judgment when the Italian police contacted her about her orphaned niece she was unable to say no and took in her little niece Natalie, Emil and Marguerite's daughter. She did not have intention to mother her. She found a nanny for her. She sold the property inherited by Natalie in Italy and the other Italian assets, opened an account in her name, and with the substantial interest paid all her expenses. Natalie was a lovely affectionate child and, despite Carla's lack of interest in her or love for her, Natalie grew attached to her and was always happy to see her. After Carla married for the third time, she talked more with Natalie because Carla spent a little more time at home. Natalie was very smart and beautiful. She was tall, had brown hair, and brown eyes. She had a lovely smile and a beautiful set of teeth and Carla thought that in a few years Natalie could become a good asset. Her new husband liked Natalie too. Natalie was more like her mother than her father. She was a good student, and she liked to care for people. She decided to become a doctor, and she specialized in obstetrics because she loved children. She looked like Emil and may be this was the main reason she kept her. However, when she thought of her sister she hated her. Was her infatuation with Emil so strong that even after so many years it had and hold upon her? Hugo Bernardi, Carla's millionaire husband, was in love with Carla and treated her like a queen. He erroneously believed that he had the right to have anything he wanted because he was rich and could afford it.

Carla showed a great interest in his business and wanted to learn to run it with him. Hugo didn't see anything wrong with it. Carla soon after her marriage left her job as manager and became the vice president first then the CEO of the company. Hugo was blessed with good health and ten years after marrying Carla he was still in good health and still very much still in love with Carla. Carla's plan was to make him fall in love with her and then kill him. However, because he was so good to her and he was such a gentleman, she kept putting off getting rid of him. She was still young and kept herself beautiful but time was going by quickly for her and she needed to be richer and in charge of his little empire.

The next year, on New Year's Eve, she met a very handsome man. He was the type of man she had always dreamed to meet. He was of medium height on the heavy side of the scale but not at all fat. He was very elegant, spoke with easy about everything. He was sociable and very rich. That night, after kissing her husband with affection, Carla told herself that the time had come to make plans for her future. Carla did not believe in hiring killers. What she had to do, she would do by herself because she could not risk discovery. She made several plans. She thought of several ways to kill him but could not make up her mind, one way or the other they were either too dangerous or too cruel. She had never loved her husband. Hugo was incredibly good to her. His death should be fast and painless. Then it came to her, she could poison him. However, it had to be an undetectable poison. She had heard about poisonous plants that that caused heart to stop, but wait a minute, Hugo was a diabetic and an overdose of insulin would do the job nicely. No, she couldn't do it safely because he was under strict medical control and his doctor could find out what she did. What can I do then, she asked herself. I had better go to the library and research poisons. Hugo was a very realistic person. He knew that he was too old for Carla. He did not trust her, so from the day he knew he was in love with her, he hired a private detective agency to check her every move.

The agency put two full time employees to keep her under constant supervision. Because Carla was in charge of the company and household finance, he arranged to pay the detective agency through his investment firm. He paid the detectives from a small account that his mother had opened for him in Switzerland. He had made it so that the monthly gains were sufficient to pay the agency fees directly from his Swiss account. Carla in all the past years had never found out about the account. Before he married Carla, Hugo stated in his will that if he died before he personally closed the account, the balance would go to a charity in Switzerland.

When he married Carla, there was no reason for Carla to know about this account.

Hugo knew everything about Carla except what her thoughts and plans were although at times he could guess what they were. Hugo knew about his wife's romance since the very beginning. He really loved Carla and he chose to pretend he was not aware of her affair because of the difference in their ages. Nevertheless, he had placed little bugs in all her clothes and rooms that enabled him to hear what she did and said. Hugo was especially interested in where his wife went with the car or what she did when she went away for a few hours. He was listening when she went to an arborist out of the area. She asked and bought some sumac poison that was undetectable and painless. The reason she gave to the arborist was that she had found bugs in her purse and did not want to smell or make the animals she intended to kill feel pain. Naturally she gave a different name wore a wig and a pair of blue contact lenses. That night Hugo made sure, he did not eat or drink at home. Carla tried to entice him to drink his special drink that she had always prepared for him at supper, but Hugo categorically refused to eat or drink because he was too full. Hugo continued, "But my love we will have supper together tomorrow night as I have bought a present for you." Carla replied, "What is the occasion if I may ask?" Hugo answered, "Oh! My little lovely princess, have you forgotten? I promise I will remind you of it tomorrow night and it will be spectacular you will see." At the next night's supper, Hugo wore his best clothes. Every night before dinner, after excusing herself, Carla absented herself for a few minutes for one reason or another. Hugo was ready for her. Before she went to call her lover, he had already filled her glass with the poisonous drink. They sat down and as was their custom picked up the glass to drink. As soon as they drank Hugo said, "I have loved you with all my heart since the first moment I saw you. I assure you that I will never touch another woman as long as I live. I promise you! Carla was feeling dizzy and very sick. She looked at Hugo and guessed the truth. She put her finger in her mouth and tried to vomit but the finger did not go far enough and she expired. Hugo made all traces of poison disappear. He began to call his wife's name loudly and with terror. The servants came running into the room while Hugo called the doctor. It was pandemonium. Hugo played the part very well because he was really in pain. He had really loved her. He was missing her already, but he could not forgive her for trying to kill him. He felt he wanted to die too and when the doctor came, he was sobbing like a small boy. As expected, the death was due to a stroke.

The news of her death got around very fast. Hugo closed the company for a week with full pay to all the employees. He arranged for the funeral. The undertaker made three rooms of the mortuary available for every-one who knew her and wanted to pay their respects. A sober sweet music played night and day for three days also. Natalie was very sad about Carla's death. She did not love her, but she was her only relative. She felt a sense of emptiness that was unexpected considering that Carla had never loved or cared for her at all. Natalie was usually alone, but now she really was alone and without a family. She went to the wake for three days. Natalie sat close to the casket looking at Carla's lovely face. She was so peaceful in that long box. They made up her face just like when she was alive and at her best. The first impression was of a beautiful woman sleeping with her eyes and her mouth closed. It seemed like she had a shadow of a smile on her overly painted mouth. Her head turned slightly sidewise, standing up she would seem alive.

Natalie for a brief moment had imagined her as someone she had seen in the past. Yes, she remembered now a face looking at her with a malicious, cruel smile for an instant a long time ago in Rome when her parents died. She had many nightmares of a woman with that face staring at her. Beginning soon after the death of her parents, even though she was a young child, she would wake up at night and would see that face slightly tilted to the right. When this happened, she would scream and start to call her mother. One night she had the nightmare while the nanny was not in the room and she screamed and screamed until Carla against her will came into the room to comfort her. Carla did her best to avoid seeing the child. However, sometimes, upon occasion, she ran into the child's room. On the few occasions when Carla had to comfort her because she was crying, the child stopped crying while intently looking at her. The look the child gave to her was not really of recognition but wonder. The encounter always shocked Carla and she could not help remembering. However, she could not believe that a three-year-old child remembered what happened that fateful night in Rome, let alone recognize her. She discarded the thought and the image from her mind. She did not see the child very often; but when she happened to see her, she would find herself staring at her wondering.

Natalie while looking at her aunt's lovely face went into a trance like state and clearly saw her aunt as the bad woman from her nightmares. Natalie awoke from her trance in terror and began to shake. She screamed, "She is a bad woman, she killed my parents a long time ago in Italy." The people who, at the time, were in the Chapel thought that she was having a fit of hysterics and looked for a doctor to help her. Fortunately, at that point, Hugo entered the chapel. He ran to Natalie took her in his arms and whispered in her ear. "Hush Natalie, you hush now. Your aunt can't do harm to anybody anymore now." Natalie fainted and Hugo, with the help of the mortuary caretaker, tried to revive and calm her "hush child, hush" Hugo repeated, "I know what she did. Unfortunately, we cannot prove it." Besides, justice has been done. Natalie fully awake now screamed, "How?" In addition, she turned her head towards Hugo, who with a very sad face looked intently in her eyes.

The Death of Thomas Carradint

Catherine Conner, upon coming home from work at about 6 AM entered apartment 132 on Caroline Street. There was silence in the house which was strange as her boyfriend Thomas Carradint was always up, waiting for her when she came home. Suddenly, upon entering the apartment, she saw Thomas' body lying on the floor. She screamed with horror "Thomas! Thomas! What Has Happened! Did you faint? Oh! My God, are you injured! Oh! Thomas, please don't die! Please don't die!" The screams of the woman were rising louder than she ever shouted before. She had reached a Hysterical tone. "I love you Thomas, I will not be able live without you." Sobbing with desperation she threw herself on Thomas's body. She hugged and kissed him as if he were alive.

There were six elegant and spacious apartments in the building. The people inhabiting the other apartments were by now all in the hall trying to enter the room. But only two women entered. They went towards the body and tried to lift up Catherine while whispering words of comfort. Catherine's sobs lessened as she was encouraged to sit down. One of the tenants asked the still sobbing Catherine if he could call the police. Catherine assented, while her sobs increased and with a piercing shrill voice she was saying "Who did this? Who could have done this horrible thing? My Thomas was as good as they come; he did not have any enemies. I will find the bastard and I will kill him with my bare hands." The sirens of the police could be heard. The sound of it made Catherine increase her sobs. Many of the tenants standing at the door began to clear the entrance. Within few minutes the police arrived. An Inspector and two policemen who started to clear the rest of the people from the door. Charles Victor, the inspector, was a tall, stocky man with a round reddish face, while the two policemen were of average height and they seemed to be very eager to start investigating.

The inspector, after looking at the body, asked one of the policemen whose name was Judd to call the homicide crew and the coroner, while Patrick, the other policemen, tried to disperse the crowd that had, now, gathered in the hall. The inspector looked again at the body for what seemed a very long time. The body on the floor lay on its back; its eyes were unmoving, blue and open. The eyes still held a look of terror and incredulity. A bloody tear had escaped his right eye and had dried on his cheek. The dead man was plump and of average height, he was wearing an elegant blue robe and blue slippers his hands were on his chest tied tightly.

It seemed as if he had tried desperately to scream or stand up. His mouth was open and blood was trickling out of it. Behind his head a wide, still enlarging stain of blood could be seen. The body had not yet reached the state of rigor mortis. The murder must have just happened a few hours back. The inspector looked all over the room. A beautiful cabinet on the left of the room contained a small television and a DVD player.

Music papers were on top of the DVD player and against the wall stood an old violin. On the back of the room there was a stained glass window with excellent designs of young girls with flower garlands on their heads like crowns. Everything in the room reflected a personality that liked order, beauty, and luxury. On the walls there were many beautiful pictures. Amongst these pictures stood like a trophy a garden picture by Monet. The room was square. It had sparse but elegant furniture. On a Mahogany table stood a bottle of water and a crystal glass, a big writing pad and a pen. A chair was half turned to the right. The inspector thought that he must have tried to get up in a hurry. He noticed that near the fourth leg of the table there was a small scratch. Catherine had stopped sobbing. The Inspector who sat beside her said "you seem to be very upset miss. Were you related to the deceased?" Catherine, crying silently, answered "I was his fiancé. We were supposed to get married in three months." She started to sob again but the inspector interrupted her. "Do you live here?" "Yes" answered Catherine. "We share the apartment; we were supposed to move into a larger one when we got married." "What was the time when you found your fiancé?" "Was he dead?" "Where did you come from?" "Please, tell me everything you know as it will help with the investigation." "I work at the casino Belleview. I sing and dance from midnight to five AM. When I came home it was five minutes past 6 AM and he was already dead. I, now, realize that I shouldn't have touched him but I was so, violently hurt. I thought that he was injured not dead". What is your name?" replied the Police inspector "Catherine Conner," exclaimed Catherine. "I will do anything to find who did this. I will be totally at your disposition." At this point the coroner and the police investigating team arrived. The Inspector got up and said "We'll continue later Miss. Conner."

The coroner, Charles Marcos, was a tall thin man of about 45 years old. After shaking hands with the inspector he went to the body of the dead man, kneeled on the floor, and started the examination. The coroner spoke with a fast and raucous voice which could not be easily understood. He took pictures of the body from all angles, and then he put in a glass container some of the dead man's blood. Then he added to another container 2 small items that were near the head of the deceased. He got up and turned towards the inspector "my job here is done" he said." "When do you think was the time of death?" asked the inspector. "Probably between 5 and 6 AM", answered the coroner. "Mr. Carradint was killed by two blows with a heavy instrument." "One blow was at the back of the head and another one flowed to top of the head, his cranium was almost split open. He died within minutes from the blows!" I have, also noted two small scratches on his left leg. The scratches may have been made by a small animal. "I will be more specific after the post mortem". "When will you know more?" asked the inspector. "Late tomorrow" he answered, and clutching his bag with both hands, he left. The police crew was still taking pictures of the crime scene. In less than an hour Mr. Carradint was removed from his house and on his way to the mortuary. Catherine, not sobbing anymore, looked at her fiancé in silence with an unmistakable expression of relief.

Catherine was a tall blonde with brown eyes. She was very beautiful. She was the typical woman that older men find interesting. She seemed to be twenty to twenty five years old, but she could have been more. Her early years were spent in too many foster homes. Her mother abandoned her at birth behind a church door and never was heard of again. At the age of sixteen she was transferred to, yet another foster home in the middle of the night to prevent further sexual abuse. This time she was placed with a well to do widow. The widow having lost her husband was afraid to be alone, she thought that a young woman would provide her with company and would give her the opportunity to help someone in need. The widow treated Catherine well, gave her a better education, and took care of her. When at the age of eighteen Catherine left, the widow gave her some money and the assurance that she would be there when and if she needed help. Despite her best attempts to find a job, she could not find one. Soon enough, she came under the influence of a pimp who led her to prostitution.

The pimp often had enforced his power over her by hitting her. He took all the money she made to the point that Catherine suffered hunger. One day after he got all her money, he bit her savagely; Catherine knifed him and ran away. She went to New York thinking that in a big city she could have lost her past. Catherine started a new life in New York. At first it was not easy. She always wanted sing and dance as a profession. She tried many restaurants and saloons always hoping to find someone rich that would love and provide for her for the rest of her life. Finally she found a job at the Café Grande, an elegant nightclub. With her beauty she had many admirers but no one seemed to be a good candidate for her expectations. A few months later she found a job with Casino Belleview where she met and fell in love with Raoul Sanchez, the head waiter. Raoul was a very handsome young man and he too was looking for riches. He did not believe in waiting for long to achieve his goal. Soon enough Raoul and Catherine became lovers He convinced Catherine to find someone rich to make their dream came true. Lately a nice gentleman was paying a lot of attention to Catherine. His name was Mr. Thomas Carradint; he was not very handsome and rich enough for her. May be he could do for a while, she thought. She flirted with him and on occasion she would let him buy her a drink. Raoul noticed the attraction of Mr.

Carradint for Catherine, and Raoul, above all, was aware of Catherine's beauty and love for her new interest. So Raoul began to encourage Catherine to spend more time with Mr. Carradint. After a while Catherine started paying more attention to Mr. Carradint. She sometimes would finish a dance or a song at his table.

One night Mr. Carradint sent to her dressing room a large bouquet of roses asking her if he could take her home after the show. Catherine returned the card to him saying that she would be honored to be taken home by him. After that day they become lovers. At first they would meet on weekends. Then after 2 months she moved in with Mr. Carradint. They were very happy, or more accurately Mr. Carradint was very happy. Catherine would meet Raoul during the day being careful not to be seen. After awhile Raoul became inpatient and wanted to rush things. He was afraid that Mr. Carradint's passion would cool down. Catherine preferred money over presents. Mr. Carradint did not give money at all. Catherine after six Months started to tell Mr. Carradint that she wanted to get married. Mr. Carradint did not like the idea of getting married. He was happy with the way things were. Catherine with joy and excitement kept telling him that a woman felt really loved and appreciated when the man she loved wanted to marry her. "You see my love a woman feels complete when she is married. There is no greater joy then when a bride wears the lovely white dress and with a veil and she walks down the aisle to the sound of bridal music. I dreamed of this day since I was a girl." Mr. Carradint answered, "Marriage is not in my plans but because is so important to you, I will marry you. Naturally we will have to draw a nuptial agreement. I did not tell you I was married before and I have a son."

"If anything were to happen to me, I will leave you well provided for, but the bulk of my estate goes to my son." "What" exclaimed Catherine "you have a son and you did not tell me? How could you! I spent all this time sucking your spit, you dirty old man!" Catherine ran out of the room and went to the kitchen where she got a heavy mallet used as meat tenderizer and she ran back to the room. Mr. Carradint still speechless was looking out the window. When he heard Catherine steps, he tried to turn towards her but a terrible blow hit him on the back of his head. He looked for an instant at Catherine who hit him again on the top of his head. He Fell on his back, for a moment he tried to get up but the only thing he could do was to put his hands in a tight fist on his chest. Was it in desperation? We will never know. Catherine coming back from the kitchen had left the kitchen door open and Suda Foo, the cat from the apartment upstairs approached Carradint's body then the cat brushed his body against Catherine's leg, she jumped and tried to hit the cat with the mallet. She did not quite hit him she injured his left leg badly. The cat screamed and ran away from the kitchen window. Catherine, terrified for what she had done, called Raoul to hide the mallet and to ask for help. Raoul arrived with his Volvo in minutes. They locked the door of the apartment to go somewhere to think and plan the best way they could escape this mess if possible. They went in a restaurant near the Café Grande. They knew most of the people and made sure to be seen by everybody. They seated themselves at a table to calm down and to think. When Catherine told Raoul about the cat he jumped out of the chair and said "you are lost woman. Not dealing with the cat was an irreparable mistake. Keep me out of it or we both will be lost. If I am out of jail, I will take care of things for you." Then he left in a hurry. Catherine went home and staged the show of having found Mr. Carradint when she come back home from the Casino Bellevue.

Inspector Victor sat, again, by Catherine to continue to ask her questions regarding the death of Mr. Carradint. "Miss Conner when you arrived home was the door closed? Was anything out of place in the room?" "Was there anything that caught your eyes as being different?" "No" answered Catherine. "Everything seemed to be quite in order. The door was closed; I opened it with my key." The inspector continued his questions. "Was Mr. Carradint expecting anybody that you know of? Do you know of anybody that would have wanted him dead?" Catherine answered "He had an affair with a woman and the woman's spouse threatened to kill him." "I think the last name was Sharinsky." The inspector took note of the information and immediately and asked his assistant at the police station to find out everything about Mr. Carradint's dealing with the Sharinskys. "Thank you for now, Miss Conner, please report to our police station after 9:00 AM tomorrow" Inspector Victor instructed her. "Now", the Inspector said, "I need to go to the other apartments to ask the tenants if anyone heard or saw anything." "I will talk with the manager first."

The manager of the building was Mr. Cavanaugh. He was an older man with a left eye that twitched. He wore decent working clothes. He invited the Inspector inside, offered to him a chair and a cup of coffee. The Inspector sat but did not take the coffee. He asked Mr. Cavanaugh if he could tell him who came and went the previous day and night from the building. "Sir, the usual people were in the building." Mr. Cavanaugh answered. "The tenants, and the tenants' friends and families were there. The delivery people are not allowed upstairs. They deliver the merchandise to the lobby, and the tenant carries whatever was delivered to their own apartment. Mr. Carradint wanted to avoid problems with unau- thorized people being in the apartment. For repairs to the apartment, I accompany the repairmen whenever they are needed. We did not have any problem since Mr. Carradint bought the building. "Oh! Inspector, this morning, early, I heard what seemed to be a painful yowling of Mrs. Thompson's cat in Apt. # 3. The cat was yowling while running up the stairs. Because the cat does this often, I did not pay much attention." "Mr. Cavanaugh would you, please, give me the names and apartment numbers of all the tenants?" The Inspector requested. "Sure, sir, immediately" Mr. Cavanaugh said. He began to write on a sheet of paper the information which he gave to the Inspector. The Inspector thanked him and went up to apartment #3. After several knocks a sleepy Mrs. Thompson opened the door. "I am Police inspector Charles Victor, Madam; I would like to talk to you about what has happened downstairs this morning." Mrs. Thompson replied "Come in, please excuse me but I was taking a nap." May I offer you a cup of tea?" "Yes, please, I would love to have a cup of tea" said the Inspector. After Mrs. Thompson had served the tea, the inspector asked her "Did you know Mr. Carradint well? Is there anything you can tell me to shed some light on his death? "I cannot say that I knew Mr. Carradint well. He was a friendly man. He made sure to wish a good day or good night to anyone of the tenants that he happened to meet. For any other needs, we have we go to Mr. Cavanaugh for help" "Do you know Miss Catherine Conner his fiancée?" "I have met her a few times but she is not the friendly type." Mrs. Thompson answered. "Do you have a cat Mrs. Thompson?" "Yes her name is Suda Foo; she is a very good companion. She wanders out at times but she always comes back home. What I don't like about her is that she likes to go to peoples' kitchens even though I feed her well. A bad habit I guess." The inspector inquired, "I heard that she was yowling last night do you know why?" "No, but someone hit her. She came home limping, there was blood on her head and she would not let me touch her. She refuses to come out from under the couch and makes a scary strange sound," answered Mrs. Thomson. The inspector called gently "Suda Foo, come here." After a while the cat's head came out from under the couch. She looked at both people, and then walked gingerly and slowly towards the inspector. The inspector immediately noticed that the right side of her body was wet with a viscous substance and that her back paw was injured as if someone had kicked her while she was running. The inspector caressed the uninjured part of her body still talking to her softly, then turning back to Mrs. Thompson He said "I have to take Suda Foo with me to be examined and find out if possible, how she came about to be injured. We will be very careful. Nothing bad will happen to her I promise you." A Reluctant Mrs. Thompson agreed. The Inspector left with Suda Foo always caressing her to keep her calm. He would meet the other tenants in the morning. Inspector Victor took the cat to the medical examiner. The cat had to be drugged to be examined and photographed. The day after Inspector Victor brought back Suda Foo to a very happy Mrs. Thompson. And he called his assistants to check on the investigation into Mr. Carradint's involvement with the Sharinskys. The officers told him that in talking to mutual friends they found out several things. Thomas Carradint was of above average intelligence. He liked the good life and young blond women. When he was drafted to fight in world war two he was 26 years old. He was married to a comely woman and had a young son. Six months after his return from the war, he divorced his wife and moved to New York. There he found a job as mail clerk. After five years he had reached the position of director of his department making enough money to buy a six unit apartment building. He moved in the one of the units, let Mr. Conrad Cavanaugh live in the second one as remuneration for managing the place. He lived a comfortable life until he fell in love with Virginia Sharinsky, the wife of the head of his mail department. She was in love with him too. They became lovers and they would meet at a motel twice a week. When Alfred Sharinsky got wind of the affair, he followed his wife to the motel to get proof of her betrayal. The next time the love birds met he tried to catch them in bed. The porter of the motel was previously paid by Mr. Carradint to give them warning so he called them. Virginia ran down the fire escape. Once Mr. Sharinsky was inside the room, the two men looked at each other with hatred and screamed obscenities at each other. They started to fight. They fought with a vengeance until they bled. In the end Mr. Sharinsky lost the fight and went home. Before leaving, while he was at the door Mr. Sharinsky turned and screamed I will kill you for this Carradint. When they questioned Mr. Sharinsky he produced evidence that he was on vacation with his wife Virginia in another state. Having ruled out the Sharinskys, the inspector returned to continue talking to the remaining tenants.

The other tenants did not have very much to add to the results of the investigation. They had not noticed anything unusual except for hearing the stressed yowling of a cat. The inspector subpoenaed Mr. Carradint's bank account records and the last month's telephone bill and upon reaching his office at the police station, he began to go through the statements. The bank statements showed the deposit from his job wages and a monthly large check to Mrs. Carradint his ex wife and son Occasionally, he would send to the same address a small check to his son, Adrian Carradint. Other checks were written to various jewelers and fashion stores. The telephone records showed many telephone calls to Catherine and two days earlier to his solicitor, a Mr. Oliver Jenkins. Other calls would be investigated later if necessary. The policemen Judd and Patrick after combing the neighborhood did not have very much to report except that a Mr. Coleman coming home from work at about 5.15 AM noticed a brown Volvo stopped at 132 Carolina Street. He did not look at the license plate number. The coroner's report stated that Mr. Carradint had died between 4 and 5 o' clock in the morning. The death was caused by 2 heavy blows on the head by a heavy object. The cat examination of his claws shows DNA, but the DNA examination was not ready yet but it would be sent to the inspector ASAP. There were numerous fingerprints in the murder room. Most of them were of the same person only two were different. The other two were those of Catherine Conner. Inspector Victor had yet, to find the weapon used by the killer. He went to the Belleview Casino to investigate Catherine. The owner of the Belleview was young, tall and thin with an amiable disposition. He answered the inspector's questions calmly and truthfully. "Catherine Conner works here am I right?" asked the inspector. "Yes, she has been working for me for a couple of years' now." replied the owner. "Could you please tell me everything you know about her?' asked the inspector. "Of course sir, but why do you need to know?" said the owner. "I am not at liberty to tell you anything at this time." answered the Inspector.

"Well then Catherine is a reliable and trustworthy person. She sings and dances beautifully and she is a good worker. She is a bit temperamental though, she flies off the handle easily. Two weeks ago I almost fired her for this reason. Because a customer spoke to her improperly she screamed and slapped him in the face. It is not that I let my employees be insulted, but I think there are other ways to put someone to his place. Other than that, I am afraid I cannot add anymore except that she was dating my first waiter, Raoul before she got engaged to Mr. Carradint, poor man, Would like to talk to him?" asked the owner. "Yes please, by the way, is there anybody else who knew her well?" The inspector asked. "I have not noticed anyone else. She kept very much to herself when she worked here." "Raoul" the owner called "can you please, come here?" Within few minutes Raoul appeared. He seemed a little nervous, the inspector invited him to seat and at the spur of the moment he asked Raoul if he drove a Volvo. "Yes," Raoul answered. "Why do you want to know?" "Because I would like to see it," said the inspector. Raoul's demeanor assured the inspector that he was implicated in the murder. Before they reached the car Raoul broke down and confessed to have helped Catherine hide the weapon in his car. "I did not have anything to do with the killing. Catherine called me and I tried to help her." When they arrived at the car Raoul took the mallet from under the left seat of the car and gave it to the inspector. The inspector said "Raoul, I appreciate your cooperation but I arrest you for complicity to the murder of Thomas Carradint" after reading to him his rights, he took him to the Police station. After the arrest of Raoul and having found the murder weapon, Inspector Victor and the two policemen that helped him with the investigation of the murder went to 132 Caroline Street to arrest Catherine Conner charging her with the murder of Thomas Carradint. The DNA confirmed that the scratch on Catherine's leg was made by Suda Foo when the cat encountered Mr. Carradint bleeding. This nailed the case against Catherine Conner completely. She had killed Thomas Carradint in a murderous uncontrollable rage.

The Woman of the Red Tavern Restaurant

*U*pon waking up Alex found it very hard to open his eyes. The bedroom window was open. The sun was shining directly into his eyes. He could see nothing but a strong red light that blinded him. After awhile he became used to the light and began to see the room. He had a strange filing. He felt that he was not alone and that someone was in the room looking at him. He sat up at the edge of the bed and looked around inquisitively. He almost screamed. On the floor nearby his bed lay the body of a woman holding tightly a large kitchen knife. "Oh my God!" He screamed with horror. He felt his hands were wet. He looked at his hands and saw blood dripping from his fingers. The body was that of a young woman. The body was sprawled on the floor. It seemed like she was dead. She was near the bed. He could not believe what he was seeing. I am having a nightmare he thought.

He instinctively rubbed his eyes thinking that he was still asleep, waking up from a nightmare, but no, he was awake. He now distinctly could see his room and the body of the woman on the floor. A little rivulet of blood was trickling down on the floor from the left ear of the body of the woman on the floor. He again looked at his bloody hands and at the knife. The blood was coagulating but still fresh. He was awake now but could not remember anything, anything at all. Still unbelieving the whole thing he put his head in his hand trying to remember. He got up went close to the body touched the carotid of her neck to make sure that she was dead, she was. He looked at the woman intensely for a few minutes but he could not recognize her. Who was she? What was she doing in his room? Then he seemed to recognize who she was, some tract of her white livid face became somewhat familiar to him. She was tall, very thin, and had blond hair. He remembered she wore long black earrings. He recognized the earrings and found it strange that he could recognize the earring; but he could not remember the woman. The situation was tragic. She wore a short red dress or was it a nightgown? Surely, she was beautiful. Then, in a flash, he remembered and recognized her. He had met her the previous evening at the red tavern singles bar. He missed his wife and even though he was tired, he felt the need to go to the restaurant that he used to go before he got married. The restaurant was the Red tavern. The Red Tavern was very large and had a long bar for single people to drink and socialize. As a restaurant it was a very good one.

The food was first class and abundant. The tables were small but not too close together. At each end of the bar there were private booths for couples to eat and be private. At the top end of the room at the other end there was a stage for people to perform. In front of the stage, there was a dance floor that was always busy. The lights from the ceiling were dim but each table had a lighted floral arrangement on the wall just above the table. The atmosphere was that of gayety and contentment. The women dressed well and some wore expensive jewels. The men wore Chino pants and no tie. The waiters were elegantly dressed in black, the waitresses wore long dresses. He noticed her because she was sitting alone at a small table reading a magazine. She seemed to be so engrossed in her reading that she seemed oblivious of her surroundings. Maybe he thought she was so alone that she seemed uninterested in what was happening around her. She was so pretty and so vulnerable. He could not take his eyes off her. He became attracted to her. So he got up and moved to a table nearby hers. She was drinking beer. Seeing him approaching, the girl composed herself. Fixed her hair and straitened her skirt. She looked at him and smiled, the moment he stopped at her table, she said, "Hello!" "Hello to you too, you are so beautiful", he replied. "You seem to be as alone as I am. Can I join you?" She replied, "Sure, please sit down." Once seated, he extended his hand and said, "My name is Alex Young. What is your name?" Jane answered him, "My name is Jane Sandrian." Jane was holding a glass of beer smiling. He thought she was more beautiful then she had looked from a distance. She had big brown eyes, blond hair and a longish pale face. She sat across him, closed the newspaper that she was holding and smiled again. Then she said, "I come here often and I never have seen you here before now." "Well!" Answered Alex with nonchalance, "This is the first time since my divorce that I came here. I have been abroad for a while to drown my sorrow. I believe I am cured! Now, I want to start a new life. I want to meet people and make new friends. I felt so lonely for the last couple of years. I love children and I want to have a family. My ex wife hated children. Oh, please, Jane, excuse me. I let my emotions get the better of me." She replied, "It is OK. I am alone too. I like to dance and drink beer." They continued to talk and drink for several hours. Alex was a tall handsome guy. He had a fair complexion brown eyes and black hair a beautiful smile and a contagious laugh. After a lavish supper Alex invited her to dance. Alex realized that, for the first time, after the divorce, he was happy. After dancing until the small hours, Alex invited her to go to his apartment. Jane who was very happy said, "Yes, but not right now. Let's dance some more." Afterwards, they went to Alex's apartment, they made love and she fell asleep.

In the morning he awoke slowly. He hurt, he did not remember last night clearly. He looked beside his bed and saw a form on the floor. It was a woman. He went over to wake her up and began to sweat as he realized she was dead. He was sure he did not know this woman that it seemed he had killed. He remembered her name and nothing else. He got dressed went in the kitchen made some coffee and drunk it absent mindedly. The clock on the wall was stopped at the number twelve that was encircled by an arc, in the arc there was a doll with big red eyes. Alex for a few second was transfixed by the clock figurine and like in flash he saw himself brandishing a knife attacking the woman he knew as Jane Sandrian. Alex after the many happy hours spent with Jane at the Red single's tavern was very happy. Then he remembered seeing Jane trying to open the top drawer of his bureau where he kept his important papers and all his money. He jumped out of bed and tried to stop Jane from opening the drawer. Jane reached into her purse, got a large knife, and tried to kill Alex. Alex stopped the knife from entering his flesh by turning the knife towards Jane's breast. Jane was still pushing the knife to kill him. Alex was the stronger of the two, so he was able to twist Jane's hand and the knife towards Jane. The twisting of the hand was so strong that her forward momentum caused Jane to run into the blade. The knife entered in Jane's breast. Alex was stunned. He was just waking up to a nightmare. He did not know what to do. He seemed to be in a trance, but he called the police. He told the 911 operator that he had killed someone that tried to kill him. The police team came almost immediately to overview the situation soon after an inspector with his assistant followed. The caller was identified, pictures were taken. The inspector and his assistant found a place to sit at a small table near the window. Inspector Amedeo Santorin introduced himself to Alex and invited him to sit down. He asked in a friendly manner all the pertinent questions related to the case. As was his custom to treat everybody with respect. He believed that it is wrong to judge anybody by the appearances in any situation. Anybody if accused of a crime is innocent until proven guilty. Alex felt much better. He was at easy speaking with the inspector. He knew that he was in the presence of an honest person. Alex recounted to the inspector in detail all that had happened. The inspector believed him nevertheless he invited Alex to go with Sergeant Butler to the police station for verification of the facts and to be fingerprinted by Sergeant Butler.

The coroner arrived soon after did not have problems establishing what had happened, It was clear from the scene that the woman died when Alex had to defend himself from her attempting to kill him. The inspector approached the coroner once he finished with the body and asked what he thought had happened from his investigation so far. He confirmed that the girl had died by a lethal knife wound to the heart. He said that from her injury to her hand from the knife guard that her hand was holding the knife that killed her. He said he would know more after the autopsy was done. But, he reminded the inspector, final determination would have to wait for blood tests to complete in a month. He would send a copy of the autopsy report after it was complete. The inspector asked the coroner to send him a fingerprint identification of the dead woman, so he could start the preliminary investigation. After relating as much as he could remember to the police, Alex checked into a hotel until the police were finished examining the scene of her death. By then he was hungry, so he thought to get supper.

Alex as he did every night since his divorce went to the Red Tavern to have dinner. This night he was upset about the previous night because of the violent end which shocked and horrified him. So, the apartment felt empty and desolate. Alex Young after a few minutes spent looking around to get acquainted with the people in the restaurant hoping to find someone likable to have his dinner with spotted a girl who was entering the restaurant. He recognized her. Her name was Emilia Carter. He had dated her before he met Angela his wife. He remembered being infatuated with her. She was very pretty. She had a mane of black hair and a sad face he felt attracted to her maybe because he was lonely. They talked about the old times reminiscing about what they did with each other back then. He looked at her and instinctively knew that he could not go back with her. After a couple of drinks at the bar it became clear to Emilia that they could not get back together again. Evidently their past marital experience had left both disillusioned. They separated as friends. The Coroner identified the woman as Laura Rivers AKA Jane Sandrian. She had been in foster care until she was an adult. She had as a child and as an adult broken arms, legs, and fingers but the injuries were not recent. She had a criminal record. He hoped that was enough to start the preliminary investigation. All recent injuries were the result of the struggle for the knife. So unless there was something in the blood work, he was going to find it a justifiable killing for Alex Young and against the dead woman. She was born in South Dakota from Mary and Roland Rivers. She was orphaned at the age of six. She was cared for her paternal grandfather who at the age of ten raped her and initiated her to a life of sex and crime. At fifteen she had become a skilled entertainer of men. Her paternal grandmother being jealous of the time and care that her husband lavished on her reported her to the social services that immediately intervened and put her with a reputable foster home. It took a long time for Laura to adjust to her new life. She escaped three times. She was caught every time the last time with dare consequences.

The last time she escaped she was caught after two days. The foster parents did not alert the Social services because they were afraid of the consequences if the service learned of her not previously reported escapades. Above all, they were concerned for the loss of income.

The foster parents decided to punish her for her last escapade in a way that she would never forget. Since they had broken the law too many times, if still she did not change, they were determined to kill her and report her as lost. They did not report Laura's escapes because the thought of losing their license terrified them. They had a big family and the husband was unemployed. So they took her to the basement tied her to a pole and beat her so much that she could not get up, from the floor, where she was left for four days. After the terrible beating,

Laura stopped running. She swore that, when alone and hurt, every night the ghost of her mother slept with her on the bare cement floor comforting her. In time her wounds healed. She had tried very hard to change her life, but she could not endure the punishment. She never forgave her grandparents and her foster parents. She loved the good life and as soon as she was eighteen, she began to live her life the way she had always dreamed. She wanted to be free and rich. Without any thought she began to live the fast life of deceit, prostitution, and crime that she had learned after her mother died.

A Father's Unforgiven Sin

Every year I use to go to visit my sister on her birthday out of town in the next State of werbena. My sister is a widow with limited financial means. She is still very young and beautiful and since the death of her husband, she has been very sad and very lonely. At twenty eighty years she is beautiful. She loved her husband very much and has a very hard time adjusting to her new life. Soon after the death of her husband, she had a nervous breakdown. I managed to visit her two to three times per month She is happy when I arrive but very sad when I came back home. The last time I visited her, she made me promise to visit her, every week. I love my sister very much but I miss my family more. I asked my husband and my daughter if my sister could come to visit us for a couple of months but they did not show much enthusiasm, they said that because we were so very happy, she would feel more the loss of her husband. I did not agree with either of them but since was for only a week that I would be absent I did not push the issue. The day before I left we went out to spend some time out to have a good time. We had a grand time. We went shopping first, and then we went to our favorite restaurant called the happy cove with the excuse that I need this short vacation every year to visit my sister during the summer I began to prepare for the trip. As every year, my daughter and my husband were very happy for me. The trip to my sister to celebrate her birthday and to be together was very important to me. My sister is a widow. She was very lonely. I went to visit with her as often as I could; and, on her birthday, I would spend one or two weeks' vacation with her. My sister works in a men's apparel factory, she lives in a small very cozy apartment near by a ski resort, we both love to ski and every year we look forward to spending a good time together. A week before my sister's birthday I started to prepare for the trip. I remember that my daughter and my husband were just as excited as I was. For me to visit her, before I departed, we gave each other a party. Despite the fact that they never volunteered to accompany me while I visited my sister I did not see anything wrong with it, may be because they seemed to care for my sister very much. I thought that they were happy for me because they knew that at least once a year my sister and I needed to be together. The fact that they never volunteered to accompany me and be with us never seemed suspicious to me because they cared so much for my sister and my happiness to be with her that I was grateful to them both.

The day before my departure, we had a little celebration. My daughter helped me pack in the morning and with my husband, the three of us left for the train station. I was very happy. It was late in the morning when we arrived at the bus station. The bus was half-full, there were many empty seats therefore, I decided to take a nap. I occupied two seats like a cot and fell asleep. Even thought my sister and I communicated with each other every day by phone, to surprise me, she didn't tell me about a surprise she had for me until I arrived at her home. Later, after supper, my sister reveled to me her surprise. She told me that she met a nice very good-looking man and accepted his marriage proposal. His name was Fred. Fred liked the outdoors very much. On the next day, after I arrived he proposed to go in the mountains to camp for two weeks. I could not possibly do that so I refused and after two days, I headed back home. I was happy to go back home. I missed my family although I was happy for my sister new happy life. I wanted her to be with her boyfriend after so many years of loneliness and quasi poverty. I hugged her with love. She wanted me to stay in her house overnight but I departed for home when they departed for camping. I thought about how lucky I was   to be able to go home early, but strangely enough, I felt a sense of foreboding. It was as if I was afraid that something was going to happen to me. The sun was shining, the birds were chirping, Everything was so beautiful, I thought, nothing can happen to me, I bet I told myself, I feel this way because I miss my sister. Once I arrive home,

I will be as happy as always to reunite with my family I could not possibly wait for my sister and boyfriend to return from their camping trip. That night I rushed home. My sister's home was on the town's outskirts and I had to catch a bus to go to the train station. I went to the kitchen to make a phone call for a cab but I impulsively changed my mind. I decided to wait for the bus that would arrive shortly. I was hoping that the short bus trip would calm me, but the thought that I would reunite soon with my family did not improve my negative disposition. I was afraid, I was nervous. I felt an incredible sense of loss that brought tears to my eyes. When it finally arrived, the bus was almost empty when I entered it. I arrived home earlier than I thought. It was almost midnight. Before heading home from the bus station, I thought to call home and let my husband and my daughter know where I was and tell them that in minutes I would be home. However, thinking that they were asleep I decided against it. I was sure that for them it would have been a pleasant surprise. When I arrived, I could see that the light in my daughter's bedroom was on. I became concerned. Why at that time of the night was my daughter's room illuminated? She must be unwell, I thought. So I rushed in the house. I heard my husband's voice; I thought he is with her, thank God. I rushed into her room. I froze at the sight. My daughter and my husband, her father, were in bed. They were actually on the bed, making love. Their happy faces looked at the door. The change was immediate their faces became like two horrified masks, for a few moments, then he pulled out from her and still naked run out from the room. I fainted. When I came to my daughter was bending over me trying to revive me. When I revived, I was incapable of speech. I decided to return to my sister's place, so I went back to the bus station and climbed on the next bus to my sister's place.

When I arrived at my sister's place, I found that they had not yet returned from their camping trip. My sister and her boy friend were not back home yet, but just outside my sister's house, I stopped for a moment to think and I realized that I could not put this heavy burden to her and her boyfriend. I decided to go back home. After walking back to the bus station, I took the first bus going back to my home. I had just sat down at a window seat. While I was still stressed and ready to cry, I heard a voice. She said, "I don't mean to pry, but if I can, I would like to help you. My name is Claudia I am alone and very angry. Can we have lunch together? Catherine was startled by the sound of the voice of the woman that sat on her left side. Catherine looked up to meet the face of a middle-aged woman. She marveled at the fact that she had not seen the woman board the bus, let alone sit beside her. The woman smiled at her and extending her hand said, "The next stop is where I get off. On the same street, there is a very good Italian restaurant. I have eaten there a few times and I assure you that it is very good. I too am alone and I would love to have company. Catherine, still somewhat put out, looked at her. The woman was very good looking and well dressed. She wore her hair long. Her face showed little age damage, only a few wrinkles around the eyes were showing. She wore her reddish blond hair loose on her shoulders. Her green eyes were beautiful, all together she was, still a beautiful woman. What Catherine found most amazing and comforting was her voice. She had a soft sweet smile and spoke with a musical tonality. Catherine listening and looking at her found that she had a calming effect on her. She felt better just looking at her. Spontaneously Catherine smiled back and said, "I will be happy to come with you, I like Italian food and I am sure that I will feel better soon thank you. As the bus stopped, because it was the end of the line, everybody stepped down and began to move to exit of the bus terminal. Catherine and Claudia headed to the main road to find the Italian restaurant. It was a rectangular and low building painted a light green color. Adjacent to a large parking lot a faire was in progress and the area resonated with loud music inviting people to engage in playing games, to buy wares, food, and sweet meats. Ecstatic children were riding the carousel and sometimes crying if the parents were not on sight. Catherine almost forgot her fears. Across the sights of the fair, the Italian restaurant mentioned by Claudia, looked elegant and inviting and both women headed towards it anticipating the pleasure of a good meal. At the entrance the hostess, who was young and beautiful, greeted them. She said, "Welcome to the garden of friendship and good food. Would you like to be seated near the window or in the middle of the dining room?" The two ladies answered in unison, "Near the window". The window was spacious and very clean. The sun at that moment was shining through the glass forming a phantasmagoric brilliance of lights and color. Suddenly, Catherine and Claudia, for a moment, were in a magic world. The voice of the hostess invited them to sit down and that brought them back to reality. However, still dazed, they examined the menu. The food on the menu was appetizing, so it did not take long for the two women to choose and order. While Waiting, Catherine began to tell Claudia about her sister's engagement and good fortune for both of them, as she could be going home earlier than planned. Though she was a little put out she was happy for her sister happiness and for the fact the she soon would be back home. Claudia, looking Catherine in the eyes said, "I am not a fatalist but I believe that for anything that happens that is out the ordinary, there is a purpose. I believe that fate made us meet. I am happy to have met you. I was unhappy to be alone, and my soul yearned to meet someone I could talk to and now that we have met and we are having lunch together, I know that we were meant to meet each other. Maybe in the near future we can be friends. I hope that in the future we can be friends". "So do I" answered Catherine. The waiter brought their food and the two women began to eat with a great spirit. The food and the wine were excellent and they ate and drank it with gusto. As often happens during and after drinking, the two women became chatty. Catherine asked Claudia about her family. Oh! My dear Catherine, I know I am rich and beautiful, but as far as happiness goes, I am very unlucky. I got married three times and three times, I got divorced. I got married to three very good looking and engaging men but they were one more dishonest than the other was. I like good-looking, handsome, tall, and well-spoken men, but not rich ones. I broke off with Walter because after six months, I found out that he was married with three children. I found out by chance. My trade is teaching. Although I am rich, I have always worked because I don't like be idle and above all I don't like to go partying. I like to dance; I like to help others when I believe I can improve their lot in life. The way I found out about him was quite strange and surprising. One day the headmaster called me to his office because a schoolmate had beaten my son at lunch. I was astonished. When I arrived I asked, "Are you sure that the headmaster asked for me?" "Yes, miss", answered the secretary, "I am." Filled with misgiving thoughts, I marched into the head master's office. The head master, in a very unfriendly way, told me, "Mrs. Gilroy, I will not tolerate your son's bad conduct in class and in the hall. If things don't improve, I will be forced to suspend him for at least one month. He is very undisciplined." The look on my face must have sent a message to head master because she stopped immediately and looked at me bewildered. I walked close to her desk and said, "Mrs. Maroni I don't know what are you talking about and looking at a unclean tall boy of about nine years old, I said, "I have never seen this child before now and I do not know who he is." The headmaster stopped talking and asked, "Aren't you Mrs. Gilroy?" "Yes, I am but this child is not my son, isn't your husband's name Gerald Gilroy? Yes, he is and still this child is not my son, At this point, the head master got up and extending her hand said, "I beg your pardon Mrs. Gilroy, I was caught by surprise, I really thought that you were the mother of this child. Forgive me." She accompanied me to the door while still apologizing. The same night when my soon to be ex-husband came home, I confronted him. He was very surprised but could not deny it. A bitter divorce followed a few months later and was the end of it. Naturally, I was very hurt and upset. At the end of the school year, I spent three months touring the Caribbean. The Caribbean countries are beautiful. I loved it there. The beaches were well groomed. The people are nice; I made many friends, and had a splendid time. Then I met Francis. He was handsome. He had a vast knowledge about almost everything. I fell for him and for one and half years we were very happy. Then I received a phone call from a woman that was a friend of Francis from high school. She informed me that Francis was her long lost husband of six years. She proved to me that she was telling me the truth. Francis was a consumed woman-izer and a very dishonest man. When he came home that same night, I confronted him. He tried to deny the whole thing but in the end, I showed him the irrefutable proof that she provided me, and he confessed. He swore to me that he loved me and he would divorce his wife and come back to me. I laughed on his face and ordered him to leave my house immediately I was so disgusted that I promised to myself that I would give up on men all together. However, after awhile I felt so lonely that I decided that I would marry an older rich man. It lasted two years, after two years I gave up on men entirely because of feeling so fed up and disgusted. Now my dear, I will not bore you with the dirty details. It must have been very hard for Claudia because she was almost in tears when she stopped. Please Catherine, if you want, tell me about you. I said, "Oh! Claudia, my story is a horrible one. It is gory and disgusting. I don't know where to begin. While waiting for the bus, I bought a gun because I have decided to kill my husband. I thought hard and long about it. The only thing that would appease me is to kill him. Claudia, caught by surprise, could not answer for a moment, and then she took Catherine's hands in hers and said, "Now honey let us talk about this. Please don't cry. You are no longer alone. I am with you. I will help you. Remember earlier when I told you that there is a reason for everything that happens to us that is out the ordinary? Now then, here we are talking like two old friends. A few hours ago we did not know that we existed and now I know that we can help each other and I assure you that we will find a way to solve, with God's help, all our problems." I replied, "No way! No one can solve my problem. I am guilty. I am a bad mother. I did not protect my little girl when she needed me the most. Where was I when she was with the monster that had sex with her and ruined her innocence? He also ruined my life forever. Why didn't I see that she needed my protection?" Catherine began to cry silently again. "Oh, honey! Please listen to me and try to calm down." Claudia said, "When a child falls down, injures his knees, and is in pain, what does he do? He cries and runs for help. He does not just stand there. He runs for help to anybody that can help him. If he does not find help, the wound festers and becomes worse. Is it not true? At this point, whatever the problem is, we have to try to find a solution. As I can see this situation, the thing to do, which is the only thing to do is to solve the problems and together we will find the best solution. Now drink your coffee and tell me everything." Catherine had listened to Claudia just like she was in a trance, then she dried her eyes; and she said, "OK we'll do it your way. I still think that the only thing I can do is to kill the monster. Your eloquence got to me, and I am willing to listen. Maybe we'll take care of the problem your way. I am tired and drained of strength. I can't even think anymore." Catherine with a very sad heart got ready to talk and tell Claudia everything. After paying the bill and giving a good tip to the waiter, they asked the waiter to recommend a private place where they could talk. The waiter said, "Of course, if you could please come with me. The waiter whose name was Alfonso took them to a small private room with a table and two chairs. Alfonso asked, "May I bring you ladies something to drink on the house?" They acquiesced, thanked him, and entered the small room. When the waiter served them, Catherine began to explain the situation to Claudia.

Catherine said, "Steven Ghepards and I married very young. I was sixteen years old and Steven was nineteen.

We met in a train on the way to school. Both of us lived in the same town, but we had never met. That day, I woke up late. When I arrived at the train station the train was already in motion, I jumped towards the only step to the entrance door, but if a strong hand had not grabbed me and pulled me in the train, saving my life and avoiding a fall that surely would have been fatal for me. The hand that pulled me to salvation belonged to a tall young man. His name is Steven. After meeting him, we fell madly in love, and about six months later, we decided to get married. I was sure that he loved me. We had a daughter. But if he loved me, he would not have fallen in love with his own daughter. I didn't look at my daughter. What I felt was a lot of pain and a need to see my sister."

I got up. I stood by the private room table crying, with my hands over my head in a tight grip. Stamping her feet on the floor, I repeatedly said to Claudia, "it cannot be. It is horrible. I refuse to believe it, my husband of twenty-five years and my daughter of fourteen have been lovers for years, practically my husband had raped my little girl indoctrinated by him to a life of sex and I never suspected anything. We were so happy; we were always in harmony and agreement about everything. The two of them seemed to adore each other and me. Their care for one another seemed natural to me. The fact that when Steven, my husband and my daughter Isabel were often close and when they gave each other a hug, what I thought, was an innocent effusion of affection and did not alarm me at all. I thought it was natural because I too hugged and kissed them very often. This has been a horrible wake up call. I feel like a ton of bricks is pressing down on me. After recovering a little, I left the private room still crying and still very much in pain. I went to a gun shop and bought a gun to kill Steven. However, before I went through with the killing, I wanted to talk to my sister to ask her to watch over my daughter because she is too young to be alone. Claudia now you know the whole thing. I went to my sister's home as soon as I returned here. She was not home. When I returned to the station, I met you." Claudia Was shocked. She, nevertheless, took Catherine's hand and looked at her with empathy. She said, "I cannot say in plain words what I feel you have gone through. You should have the right to kill the animal. I think that if I was in your place, I would feel what you feel, and I would like to kill him too. However, think of your daughter, she is innocent. She was a child when he raped her. I can only imagine the lies he must have told her at the beginning. I can only imagine the way he acted and the gestures he made to her. Children, naturally, like sex. I am sure she is scared out of her mind now. If you kill your husband, the poor girl will be alone and go to some foster home to live a life of neglect and despair. Do you want that for your little girl? She was too young to understand and know what was happening. Please, honey, give me your gun. We will report him to the police. So he will never come close to your child again. Don't be too hard to yourself. You loved and trusted him and no one in a million years could have suspected that something like that could ever happen. Your love for both of them and the natural intimacy between a father and his daughter hid it from you. Your daughter needs you to restore her life and faith. After he is no longer available, you are the only one that can advise her and she can trust. In doing so, you will save the life of your little girl. We all know that there are bad and good people in our world. You and I have met bad people so far. Nevertheless, we don't have to despair; we are going to wait for happiness to reach us. We are going to open our hearts to hope. Catherine was not convinced, but she gave the gun to Claudia and began to cry again. Now, there was hope and thankfulness in her tears. She began to relax because she had to be there for her daughter.